Leaf Me Alone

Julie B Cosgrove

Write Integrity Press, LLC

Leaf Me Alone
© 2020 Julie B Cosgrove

ISBN-13: 978-1-944120-86-3

Published by Pursued:
an imprint of Write Integrity Press, LLC
PO Box 702852
Dallas, TX 75370

Find out more about the author, Julie B Cosgrove, at her website: www.juliebcosgrove.com
or on her author page at www.WriteIntegrity.com.

Printed in the United States of America.

Dedication

To all who provide care for those
facing the end of their lives.

*Therefore, as we have opportunity, let us do good to all
people, especially to those who belong to the family of
believers.*

Galatians 6:10

Chapter One

Shannon Johnson's heart jittered a bit. "The twinkle in her eyes has disappeared. It's always there, reflecting her smile. That seems to be missing, too."

"Who?" Her husband, Jayden's, face scrunched as if he'd just sucked a rotten lemon.

"Grace Perkins." Shannon motioned with her head toward the corner of the café where an older lady sat alone, hugging a mug and staring into nothing.

Jayden angled his eyes to view the bent-shouldered woman through the heads of the other diners. "The one whose face is as white as her hair?"

Shannon touched his arm. "Yes. She's always so upbeat. Maybe I should check on her."

He swung back to face her, his expression still puzzled as if she'd asked him to spell the word *elephant* in Chinese. "You know her?"

Did he just ask her that? How could he not recognize the name of the lady who had been her mentor for the past two years? Surely, she'd mentioned Mrs. Perkins tons of times. Did he not listen? She sucked in a breath. "She leads the Bible study Bailey, Jessica, and I take, hon. Last year it was on Matthew. This year we are doing John."

"Ah." Recognition lit his face, at last. He pecked Shannon's cheek, "Go see to her, girl."

"You think?"

Jayden stood and pulled out her chair. "Take your time. If there is anything I can do, let me know."

Warmth oozed up from Shannon's heart into her soft, milk chocolate face. Since Jayden drove a long-haul rig, he was gone most of the time. They rarely spent more than two days together and hadn't gone out to eat for months. Yet he must have detected the anxious concern in her voice, and the desperation on the older woman's face. Okay, she'd forgive his momentary lapse of memory.

"You're the best hubby ever." Shannon squeezed his ebony fingers as she rose from her seat.

He waggled his head. "About time you figured that one out." His deep, grizzly bear-colored eyes flickered with laughter.

More like a giant teddy bear. Shannon playfully punched his arm then slipped through the crowded restaurant, white-noised with human chatter. She slid into the empty bistro chair next to Mrs. Perkins. The woman didn't stir. Her blank focus remained on something only she could perceive.

"Mrs. Perkins?" Shannon laid a gentle hand on the woman's bony arm. "Everything okay?"

Clouded blue eyes blinked. The old lady half-turned her head, her eyes still seeking something across the room. The answer barely escaped her wrinkled lips. "No."

What? Not the response Shannon expected.

So many people leaned on Mrs. Perkins for inner strength. She'd borne every burden, yoking her faith to others when they weakened and leading many more to a deeper conviction through her Bible classes. She oozed steadfast faith from every pore. Until now.

The window into her mentor's humanity had cracked open, but the air filtering in felt stale, not fresh. Icy tingles prickled through Shannon's chest. She pressed her hand to it.

The always cheerful, positive woman with the wisdom of Job slumped a tad further in her chair. Her glance shifted to the tablecloth as she set her mug down. Then, Mrs. Perkins jolted as if a cold breeze kissed her face. Had she realized that she'd let her guard down, if only for a nanosecond? She shook herself and faced Shannon full-on with a small smile. "But God is still on His throne, my dear."

Typical Mrs. Perkins response. Good to hear, but the platitude didn't erase the concern Shannon felt. She swallowed and straightened her shoulders. "Yes, ma'am. He is." Shannon slid her hand over the woman's fingers, afraid to love-squeeze them in case the bulging knuckles cracked. When did Mrs. Perkins become so frail? "God knows your plight, but can you let *me* know so I can pray for you?"

A smirk seeped into the eighty-two-year-old pasty cheeks like warm butter into hot oatmeal. "You listened in class last week."

"I always try. You've taught me so much over the past two years."

"I'm glad. It's been my pleasure to teach you." Mrs. Perkin's eyes glistened with a microscopic spark of the twinkle they usually held. Then they clouded again. She leaned closer. "Shannon, I won't be attending services at Holy Family Bible Church much longer."

"You won't? Why?" Grace Perkins belonged at that church as much as the walls and floor.

"Soon I'll be going home."

"Are you moving back to Florida where you were raised?" Shannon knew the woman hadn't always lived in the San Antonio area. All who took her classes heard about the wonderful life-lessons she'd learned growing up on the Gulf Coast near Fort Meyers during World War II.

"No, dear." Tears floated in her lids, but now a soft and solid peace oozed across Mrs. Perkins's crinkled face. "I mean my real home. Forever. I'm dying."

The room became frigid and sweltering at the same time. Shannon gave her body a shudder as if to sift the statement into her brain.

"I . . . I don't understand." Shannon gulped back the shock clogging her throat.

"We all do pass on, you know."

"Yes, but . . . who will lead the Bible study now?" As soon as the question left her tongue, Shannon cringed. How selfish of her to think only about God yanking this dear woman from her life.

Mrs. Perkins's eyes softened as if to indicate she understood. The woman lived up to her name, extending grace to everyone she encountered. "Angela Bayberry will. She has been my assistant for over ten years. You recall she led the study last year when I fell and wrenched my back."

"Yes, I do. Of course." A moment of silence hung between them. Shannon pursed her full lips together and wondered if she should ask the next question. The "how long do you have" one nobody should really mention.

The astute woman winked. "The doctors say I have another three to four weeks, but I'm leaving the details up to God. In the meantime, they insist I check into hospice this afternoon."

"Hospice? Weeks?" The words swirled through her mind like an egg on one of those titanium-coated frying pans the infomercials hocked. She couldn't make them stick.

But another thought surfaced. Why did Mrs. Perkins confide in her? Her faith resembled a mustard seed compared to the elms and oaks that grew in the garden of the Lord's known as Holy Family Bible Church.

She must have spoken the question out loud because the woman cocked her head. "Because, my dear, you stopped to ask. I have been sitting here praying on whether I should let anyone know. My pride didn't want all the attention. But you heard the Holy Spirit's whisper and came over."

Shannon blinked. "I did?"

"You are listening to Him more. I can tell. I've noticed the light shining in your face as we've studied the Bible. It is filtered through some pain but also triumph, even at your young age." She patted Shannon's hand before returning her own to her coffee mug.

Shannon sat back. Thirty-one didn't seem young to her at all. In fact, she had begun to feel a tad bit old. Her biological clock had begun to tick, but with Jayden on the road so much, babies were not in their plans.

"You're married, Shannon. You understand life a bit more than Bailey and Jessica." The woman turned her head toward the front of the café.

Shannon's eyes followed Mrs. Perkin's gaze.

Bailey stood at the entrance with Chase, the new chief detective of their small town. Raised next door to each other, they had rediscovered their unexpressed feelings during a case involving a fifty-year-old mystery in Bailey's family. Jessica came in with them.

Jessica now lived in Tulsa most of the time in order to help convict the men who had wrongly accused her late father, which had led to his imprisonment. Shannon and Bailey suspected Jessica also wished to spend more time with Grady, the handsome district attorney who had helped bring her father's innocence to light after his death.

"Your two friends are sweet, and I know they believe in our Lord, but they are too wrapped up in the tangles of new love. They have turned inward, as they should, to concentrate on what's developing between them and the men God's brought into their lives."

The three waved to Jayden. He half-raised from the table, motioning for them to join him. Tall, dark, and handsome with the physique of a linebacker. Shannon's heart leaped as it did six years ago when they first met.

"You have a fine man, my dear. Hold tight to him."

"I plan to." Shannon grinned, first out of love for her man, then wider when she realized Mrs. Perkins had shifted the topic. She shook her finger at the eyes shielded by rhinestone glasses. "But that doesn't answer my question."

The old woman nodded. "You mean the question inside the question. You want to do more than just pray, correct?"

"If I can. Of course."

"How long is that fine man-ox of yours gonna be in town?" Her tone held no condemnation, only admiration.

"Until this evening, then he heads out on the road again. Why?"

"Will you two help me settle in? I have no family here."

"Um . . ." Not many people would call Shannon Johnson a woman of few words, but at this moment her brain became thick mush, sinking her response somewhere away from her tongue.

Mrs. Perkins wiped away the suggestion with her hand as if erasing a blackboard. "Never mind, dear. You two need every second you have together. I can ask Pastor."

Shannon's heart fell to her big toe. "Oh, no. It's fine. Truly. It's only that I'm surprised you'd ask me, of all people."

The elderly Bible teacher clicked open her purse and rummaged through it for a small notepad and pen. With a shaky hand, she scrawled her address, tore off a sheet, and handed it to Shannon. "Here is my address. I will see you both at two?"

Shannon folded the note and slipped it into her skirt pocket as she rose. "We will be on time." She leaned in. "Promise."

Several times, Shannon had snuck in a few minutes late to class. Having her own pet and plant care business demanded a lot of time. Mrs. Perkins had always acknowledged her with a smile, but also with a glance at the clock. Message received.

"Good." Mrs. Perkins gingerly rose and laced her purse handle through her arm as she grabbed her cane.

Shannon extended her elbow to assist her.

"I'm fine. I can walk." She began to wobble away then turned back. "There may be something else I will ask of you two. But first I need to pray on it some more."

Okay? Shannon stood in silence as the elderly lady shuffled to the cash register. Then she weaved her way back to her husband and friends. Chase, Bailey, and Jessica chatted as they scanned the menu. Shannon slid into her seat and sipped her room-temperature coffee.

"Well?" Jayden's thick brows pushed together.

Shannon captured his gaze, willing her chin not to quiver. "I'll tell you later."

"Tell him what? Or should I even ask?" Bailey folded her menu and laced her arms over her placemat.

Tears fogged Shannon's eyes. Should she confide in her dearest friends and her husband, who now rubbed small circles across her upper back, or keep it to herself?

"Honey? What's wrong?" Jayden drew closer.

Shannon sucked in a deep, shaky breath. Mrs. Perkins hadn't specified that she wanted her condition kept quiet. But she hadn't exactly announced it in church today either. She took another sip of coffee to stall before answering him.

The concern on the four pairs of eyes gazing at her wouldn't be squelched unless she said something. She set the mug down and ran her forefinger around the rim. "Mrs. Perkins is leaving Holy Family."

Jessica slapped her hands to the table. "No. Really? I thought the only way she'd leave is in a pine box."

Shannon gasped. *Did Jessica just say that?* Tears welled, threatening to trickle down her cheeks. No, not here. She wouldn't cry in public.

"Excuse me." She pushed back her chair. It toppled to the floor in an echoing crash. *Oh great. Now I have the whole restaurant's attention.*

Shaking like an abandoned kitten on a cold rainy day, Shannon dashed to the ladies' room, sensing everyone's eyes on her back.

She shoved the door open with all her might. A quick glance confirmed the place stood empty. With a sigh, she clutched the faux marble countertop to keep her knees from crumbling. How could God call this wonderful woman home? Okay, sure. She was in her eighties, but more and more people were living well into their nineties. Didn't He know how much they all needed Mrs. Perkins in their lives?

"Please don't take her, Lord. Not yet." A warm tear trickled onto her face.

"Take who, Shan?"

Shannon jolted. She hadn't heard Bailey slip in. Of course, her friend would come check on her. She blinked away the tears from her mascara.

Bailey's hand gripped her arm. Then her breath hitched. "Not Mrs. Perkins?"

Shannon nodded and raised her gaze, her eyes scanning Bailey's face for her reaction.

"Oh, my word." It escaped her friend's mouth in a hoarse whisper.

The restaurant noise outside grew louder. Shannon turned to see the door open as Jessica stood in the wedge of fluorescent light. Jayden peered around her friend, his hand massaging the back of his neck. A sure sign he felt helpless to fix whatever upset his wife.

"I'm okay." Shannon swiped her cheek. "Jayden, bring me a glass of water, please. I'll explain it to you in a minute. First, I want to talk to Bailey and Jessica about what Mrs. Perkins confided in me."

"Okay." A slight expression of hurt flitted across his eyes.

"Thanks, hon. You're the best." She forced a wide smile. She truly loved him. But truth be told, most of the time he traveled. Whenever Shannon needed advice or comfort, she turned to her two best friends. Maybe not how it should be, but . . .

Jessica slipped in, eased the door closed, and leaned her backside against it as if to barricade anyone else from entering. "What's going on?"

Dabbing a damp paper towel on her face, Shannon answered her question, avoiding eye contact. "Mrs. Perkins will be in a pine box, Jess. The doctors say in three to four weeks."

Jessica slapped her hand to her open mouth. "Oh, I didn't mean . . . I was joking . . . I . . ."

Bailey grabbed their hands. "Time to lift this upward, ladies."

The three bowed their heads, whispering their thoughts, as tears slid down their cheeks to puddle on the scuffed linoleum floor.

Chapter Two

Jayden stood in the hallway, a glass of water in his hand, bewildered as a sparrow after flying through an open window into a house.

Shannon exited the ladies' room and took it from him as she whispered a thank you.

His eyes darted to the reddened eyes of her friends who appeared behind her. "Ladies? What's going on?"

His wife took a long gulp and set the glass down on a tray holding a few other dirty dishes. "Mrs. Perkins gave me some bad news."

She hooked her arm through his. Her fingers felt icy. Not a good sign. He covered them with his hand. "Which means?"

"Come on. I'll explain in the car. Let's settle the bill."

"I already paid and left a tip. I figured you were through eating."

Shannon rubbed his forearm. "Thanks."

Her voice sounded stronger but still a bit shaky. She brushed past him.

At first, his legs didn't want to move. He wanted to jerk her back into the ladies' room, hoping no one else would come in, and demand she explain. But he'd learned long ago that she despised drawing attention to herself. He blew a breath out his nose and followed her back into the buzz of the café.

As they passed, Jayden leaned into Chase's ear. "It's cool, man. Something about their Bible study leader getting bad news." His head motioned behind him. "Bailey and Jess will be here in a sec."

Recognition passed between them in male telepathy. Women. Who could figure them out? Especially those three. At times it seemed as if their three hearts wound together in conduit like electrical wires to a breaker. One spark and they all flickered.

He pushed the glass door open and allowed his wife to exit first. The bright midday sun slammed his senses. San Antonio hung in the aftermath of a late Canadian blast which had plummeted temperatures in a matter of hours from a balmy 70 to 39 degrees. Quickening his pace, he clicked the fob to open the doors of their subcompact. "Get in, Shan. It is still freezing out here."

She managed a forced grin. "Right? And to think next

week is spring break. Those kids at the coast will be like popsicles."

Great, now their conversation had shrunk to the weather like two strangers on a first date.

She settled into the passenger seat and reached for the safety belt without any further comment. He let out another drawn-out sigh as he closed the door. His wife tended to bottle her worries like thickened ketchup, which made her outburst in the café even more disturbing.

Jayden rounded the back of the car, opened the driver's side door, and slid behind the steering wheel. Before he pressed the ignition button, he swiveled to face her. "Okay, hon. What's going on?"

Shannon gave him a weak smile. "Thanks for waiting until we left. And for the water. I didn't mean to ignore you, but Mrs. Perkins is, well, sort of a bond for Bailey, Jess, and me. None of us have grandmothers anymore, so I guess we've kinda adopted her."

He covered her slender fingers with his. "I get it. Women need women." At least he tried to understand. It still hurt that she always seemed to turn to her friends first.

"She wants our help."

"So, you are taking off with them this afternoon?" Keep it even, man. Whatever it is, it's important to her. Don't let your disappointment show.

"No, Jay. Mrs. Perkins needs *us*. You and me."

Her words caught his breath. She may as well have dumped a pitcher of iced tea across his chest. His eyes widened so quickly, he felt his skin stretch. "I don't even know her."

Shannon slid her hand from his and ran it up and down her safety restraint. "Well, she sort of knows you. There have been a few times . . ." She stopped. "Like you said. Women need women."

Another frigid wave washed over him. "Are we okay?"

She unclicked her seat belt and slid across the console into his arms. "Yes, sweetie. Of course, we are."

She nestled into his chest, making him tingle with desire, as much emotionally as physically. He encased her in his embrace and kissed the crown of her head.

"Please talk to me."

"You, Jayden, a man, are asking me to talk?" She let off a sweet scoff as she raised up.

He cupped her chin. "Yeah, but keep it between us, okay? I'd hate to lose my man card."

That brought a half-smile. Then her face stiffened again. "I will. And I'll explain everything as you drive." She settled back into her bucket seat.

His arms suddenly ached with emptiness as his wife's warmth dissipated from them. "Yes, ma'am." Irritation laced his response and he knew it. Clinching his teeth, he started the engine.

Shannon flashed him a frown as the warning emoji to buckle up appeared on the console. It let off an annoying, urgent ding-ding-ding. She tugged on the restraint to re-click it. "Okay, okay, you bossy car. I'm doing it. Hang on."

Suddenly they both sputtered out a laugh. He leaned in to give her a long kiss.

"People are staring at us through the café window." Shannon pulled back with a smirk. "Let's leave. I don't want to give them any more of a show without charging them."

"Got it." He twisted to the rearview window to check for traffic before pulling out onto the street.

They drove in silence for a block—a long block. He almost heard the Jeopardy show tune in his mind as his finger tapped the steering wheel. Then a wise voice filtered in. *Give her time. She'll spill when she's ready.*

An audible hiccup, then a long sigh broke the stifling quiet. "Mrs. Perkins is moving into hospice this afternoon."

"Wait. Hospice? Does that mean . . ."

"Yeah, it does." She lowered her gaze to her hands.

He strained to see if new tears formed in her deep russet eyes, but they remained dry. "I see. What does she need us to do for her, girl?"

"She has no family and has asked us to help her haul

her belongings over there. We are to be at her place this afternoon at two." She fished out a note with a scrawled address on it. "I'll plug it into the GPS."

He glanced at the digital time display on their dashboard. 12:18 p.m. "Is it too cold to go to Lover's Point first?" He lifted one hand from the steering wheel and ran his finger down her cheek.

"Not if we stay in the car with the heater going and use the blanket in the trunk." She winked and took his hand in hers.

His heart leaped as his thumb traced her wedding ring. Man, he missed this lady when he was on the road. That eighteen-wheeler cabin could get awfully lonely, and the long hours behind the wheel were getting old, fast. Good money, but he needed to find a job that kept him home more often. As he turned onto the narrow dirt road leading to the spot overlooking the lake, he sent up a small prayer asking God to help him find one.

The Johnsons pulled into the senior living community at 1:56 p.m. Shannon never liked coming to these places. It rubbed the reality in her face that one day this would be her future. Wheelchairs, oxygen tanks, and a tasteless, salt-free dinner at four in the afternoon.

Jayden rolled down his window to speak to the security guard. "Mr. and Mrs. Jayden Johnson to see Mrs. Grace Perkins. She's expecting us."

He nodded and wrote their names on his clipboard. "You two helping her pack up?"

"Yes, sir. She goes to our church."

"Give her my best wishes. We'll all miss her."

"Sure thing."

He waved them on as the gate creaked open. "Turn right at the stop sign, then take the second left. She is two doors down. Number 182."

"Thanks." Jayden pressed the button to raise the window. He let his foot off the brake and eased the car through the opening.

Within a few minutes, they pulled up to the curb. Mrs. Perkin's residence resembled every other one stacked side by side like retired soldiers weary from battle. Red brick with dirty-white shutters. A short sidewalk, ending in a handicap ramp, led to the small front porch. The last of the grass daisies and a few dandelions peppered the barren lawn, browned in spots by the arctic blast.

As they exited the car, the screen door squeaked open. Mrs. Perkins, her cardigan wrapped tightly around her, motioned to them. "Right on time. Please, come in. Come in."

Shannon resisted the urge to rush to her and encase her in a bear hug. Part of her wanted to squeeze the cancer, or whatever disease ate the woman's body, right out of her. God did still heal, right? She'd seen the videos and heard the missionaries from Africa testify to it. Would He work through her if she prayed hard enough?

Mrs. Perkins's face softened as a familiar, telltale wisdom sparkled in her eyes. "It's all right, dear Shannon. I'm at peace now." She nodded to Jayden. "But before you gather my things, I do want to speak to you. Both."

She padded across the threadbare oriental rug that obviously had been a part of her life for a long time. Her dimly lit living room pulled Shannon into the past. Furniture from the 1980s crammed the space, speckled with knick-knacks and memories. The woman shuffled to a mahogany, three-tiered table laden with framed photographs and figurines. Two cardboard boxes sat on the floor beside it.

Were they to pack up all this stuff now . . . or later, after she . . . Realization of the inevitable plummeted to Shannon's stomach. She glanced at Jayden who flashed her a feeble smile. Did he think the same thing?

Mrs. Perkins waved her bird-like hand. "Please sit. Do you want some hot tea? Still nippy out there, isn't it?"

Jayden shot a glance at Shannon. Obviously, he wanted her to answer for both of them.

"No, ma'am. We're fine." She edged onto the sofa and motioned for her husband to do the same. A faded, olive-green recliner with a lace doily draped on the back sat across from them, angled toward the picture window. Next to it stood a walnut table laden with a Bible, a tissue box, and the daily crossword puzzle from the local newspaper.

"Very well." The older woman picked up a framed photo from the tiered table. She handed it to Jayden. Shannon leaned in to peek. A black and white picture, faded with age, revealed a young boy with a faraway, forlorn expression.

"That's Manuel Andersen. He's my nephew. I raised him. His father, my brother David, eloped with a Cuban girl he'd met at a club in Miami where his band played. Manny appeared nine months later. May 2, 1957."

Shannon glanced at Jayden. Why did Mrs. Perkins tell them this?

With a blank expression, he handed it back to the woman.

Mrs. Perkins polished the smudges from the frame with her sweater sleeve. "They basically handed him to me and my husband when Manny turned two."

"Why?" Shannon blinked. How could people abandon their own kid?

"Left to travel the world with the band. Last we ever saw of them." She shook her head and returned the photo to its place.

Jayden's forehead wrinkled. His eyes held the same question as Shannon's. Why reveal this to them?

"Manny always was a moody child. After my Henry died in Vietnam in 1968, I could never control him, and he didn't want anything to do with church or God. Always got into fights at school. Spent hours upon hours in his room." She waddled over and eased her bones into the recliner. "The day he turned eighteen, he got a birthday card from his wayward parents with a hundred-dollar bill in it. No return address. Manny threw it on the floor. I'd seen him moody, but never angry like that."

She motioned to her heirloom furniture. "He toppled that tier table with all the family photos on it and stomped out. I can still hear the crash in my head. I got a postcard a week later from Jacksonville. He'd joined the Navy. He never contacted me again. I'm not sure he is still alive."

Shannon realized her mouth hung open. She shut it quickly. She had no idea such heartaches laced her Bible study teacher's past.

Mrs. Perkins reached into her skirt pocket for a yellowed newspaper clipping. She unfolded it and motioned for Shannon to come take it. "Years later, I got this."

Shannon glanced at the front page of the Fort Meyers News-Press, dated July 18, 1988. She read the headlines out loud. "Local Man Robs Liquor Store. Clerk Killed. Police Conduct Manhunt."

A mug shot, obviously from a driver's license or military ID, showed the face of a thirty-something man. He wore the same pouty expression as the photo of the boy.

"Yes, it's Manny. An old neighbor from Fort Meyers sent me the clipping several years ago. She discovered it when she unpacked some things from storage that she'd wrapped in newspaper." She wiggled to the edge of her easy chair. "I know nowadays you can find stuff on computers, but I never learned to use one."

"So, you want us to see what we can find out?" Shannon passed the clipping to Jayden.

"I want you to locate him if he is still . . ." She glanced away for a minute. "I really want to see him one more time before the Lord calls me home. He's my only kin."

The expression in Jayden's eyes indicated it was her decision to make. Of course. Because he'd be on the road again, leaving her and her friends to investigate what had happened. As always.

"But, why us?"

The wise old woman folded her arms into her lap. "You helped Bailey find her long-lost aunt. You played a part in helping Jessica exonerate her father for a murder he didn't commit. And I recall you saying Jayden did long haul runs between here and Miami, so . . ."

Shannon shook her head. Jayden didn't have time to flit all over Florida. "Mrs. Perkins, I . . ."

Jayden rose from the couch. "Of course, we will do everything we can to help locate your nephew. Put your mind at ease and put your trust in the Lord to guide us, Mrs. Perkins."

What did he just say? Shannon felt the blood drain from her face. Did that mean he didn't plan to leave tonight?

"May we take the photo as well? I'd like to make copies of both it and the news clipping."

Hope glittered in the old tired eyes. "Of course. And his birth certificate is in the strongbox on my bed." She pointed a crooked finger toward a short hallway. "Bring it to me and I'll retrieve it for you."

He folded the news clipping and placed it in his shirt pocket, then headed in the direction she indicated.

Shannon's eyes followed him as he left the room, then returned to her mentor's softly wrinkled face. "You want me to ask Jessica and Bailey for help?"

She lifted herself from the recliner with her cane and wobbled back to the photo display. "Of course, my dear. You three are a team. But I don't want everyone to know about my condition. Pastor knows, as does Angela Bayberry and the prayer team. Now you three and your dear husband. He seems very capable and trustworthy. You chose well."

"I think so, yes, ma'am." Shannon ran her hands over each other, still puzzled at her husband's eagerness.

Her mind swirled as she watched the old woman's fingers shakily remove the photo from its frame. Another missing person? Possibly a criminal? Did Manuel Andersen really murder the clerk? Had he ever been caught? If so, would he still be in prison thirty years later? And would they let him out, much less cross the state line, to visit his dying aunt? Not likely. Why had Jayden, her level-headed man, jumped to take this on? Only to break Mrs. P's heart.

Her stomach flipped, half in excitement and half in trepidation. Wait until Bailey and Jessica heard about this. It seemed as if they'd become genealogy mystery magnets. Maybe they should start their own business. Hang out a sign. Post it on social media. Got an unsolved case involving your kin? Call on us.

The mantle clock ticked a little too loudly as they both waited in silence for Jayden to return. At last, she heard his shuffled stride coming down the hallway. He entered the front room with the box and handed it to their hostess.

Mrs. Perkins fumbled with the lock. She took so long, Shannon resisted the urge to yank it from her and pry it open. Jayden remained standing with his hands folded in front of him. He had a patient streak Shannon always admired.

At last, the lid released with a slight creak. Mrs. Perkins dug through the box with her arthritic fingers. "Ah, here it is. I knew I still had it."

Jayden smiled as he took it from her.

The old lady motioned around the room with her eyes. "The Wounded Vets Association will come tomorrow morning to collect all the furniture, dishes, my clothes, and linens. I've boxed most of it up. All we need to gather are these few knick-knacks and my Bible to take with me. My suitcase and toiletries are already packed."

After they helped Mrs. Perkins box up the rest of her memories, they carted her to the hospice facility and then rearranged her meager possessions in her room. A nurse tapped at the door and entered with a vital signs machine. Time to leave.

Shannon and Jayden said their goodbyes. Shannon gazed down at the shell of the woman she admired for being so strong and active despite her age. Now the bed seemed to swallow her like a cocktail wiener in a hot dog bun.

"I will drop by to see you in a day or so."

"That would be nice, dear. But finding Manny is more important."

Shannon leaned to kiss her mentor's leathery cheek, and then let Jayden lead her out. They walked down the corridor in silence and through the front double doors into the late afternoon sun. It hadn't warmed the earth very much. But being out of the dismal environment released a burden from her chest.

"I pray to God neither of us will ever end up here."

"Not for us to decide, girl." He clicked the fob and opened her car door. Always the gentleman. May he keep doing it well up into their eighties. She cleared her throat to thank him and slid in. But his eager-beaver attitude still puzzled her. Jayden never did anything without mulling it over first.

After he had fastened his belt, she turned to him. "Why did you agree so fast to help find Manny?"

"I wanted to ease the old lady's mind. She has enough on her plate, hon."

"You lied to her? Jayden, that's not like you."

He turned on the engine. "I didn't lie. I told her we would do what we could. I'm just afraid it won't be very much."

She knew it. "Because you have to get back to work?"

"That and because it's a cold trail. What can you, Bailey, and Jess accomplish? Bailey is an accountant. Jess a freelance writer, and you run a pet and plant sitting company. None of you are skilled in this type of thing."

She narrowed her eyes. How little he knew of what had happened the past few years while he drove back and forth across the country. Bailey ended up reuniting family members who had shut each other out of their lives for five decades. Jessica had courageously helped solve a thirty-year-old murder. Why couldn't they locate this guy? "You don't think we are capable, do you?"

Jayden kept his eyes on the road. "Look, girl. I don't mind you and your friends doing some online research, but let's face it. Chances are the guy already went to the electric chair, or whatever it is they use in Florida. We're talking more than thirty years ago."

Shannon stared out the side window. "You're right, as usual. But even so, if there is a small chance . . ." She swiveled back to face him. "That woman has done so much for everyone else. I want to do this for her."

One eyebrow lifted. "Do you? You seemed to be the hesitant one back there in her home."

"I know. I don't doubt we can determine what happened to him. That's not it."

"What then?"

"It seems we keep stumbling into circumstances involving criminals. We might as well open a detective agency. Maybe I should call my business Pampered Pets, Plants and Practical Probes." She huffed and wove her arms over her chest.

Jayden's laugh bounced off the upholstered car roof. "That's a mouthful." He reached into his pocket. "Do me a favor. Take these originals. Make copies. Talk it over with your friends, and possibly Chase Montgomery. Pray on it, and then call me in a few days. We will discuss it more then."

He reached for her hand as he gazed out the windshield, his other fist gripping the wheel. "Then, if you and your friends decide to pursue this, I'll see what I can do to help."

He kissed her fingers as he turned onto the highway that led to their apartment.

"Really?"

He jerked his head back to face her. "Of course. This lady means a lot to you. Don't you think I know that?"

She saw him swallow hard as he returned his attention to the traffic. She'd probably bruised his ego by questioning if he'd be there for her. Poor guy. All her angst melted to the floor mat. She thanked God for bringing this man into her world even if he did scrape her nerves now and then.

But each time he left, it made the goodbyes harder and harder to handle. This time would be no exception. Why couldn't he find a good job in south central Texas?

Leaf Me Alone

Chapter Three

Mrs. Perkins jolted from a fitful sleep. Did she hear footsteps in her room? She held her breath and lay very still.

Soft breaths accompanied the light steps. Nursing shoes? Yet no one announced themselves. She heard no squeak of the vital signs machine's wheels. Who could it be?

The steps came closer to her bed and stopped. She felt a presence hover over her and willed herself to stay still and calm. No need to panic. Maybe they wanted to make sure the sleeping pills they'd made her swallow did their job.

No way would she admit she'd spit them out later. She hated medications. Always had and took pride in the fact she only took two every day—a statin and a blood pressure pill. And an occasional aspirin. Most of the people her age carried around little boxes full of this and that to take morning, noon, and night.

After a few minutes, the footsteps moved away. Mrs. Perkins heard the hinges on the door move. The wedge of light shining against the wall narrowed to a sliver again.

She sighed out the breath she'd been holding. Oh, why wouldn't her doctor let her die at the apartment where she'd lived for over two decades, surrounded by friends her age and all of her memories?

She drew her pillow tighter as she prayed. "Please let Shannon and her friends find Manny. It's all I ask."

"So, what do you think?" Shannon gazed at her friends.

Jessica, Bailey, and Shannon sat cross-legged around her coffee table after Bible study, which had been flat and somber despite Angela Bayberry's upbeat voice. Everyone missed Mrs. Perkins. When Angela had stated at the beginning of class that their leader had been under the weather, the three had shared glances and pressed their lips together.

Now, surrounded by several photocopies of the newspaper article and the old photograph, they concentrated on their mentor's request. Shannon had placed the originals in a plastic baggie to be tucked away in her sock drawer.

"I don't know, Shan. We don't have a lot to go on." Bailey shrugged.

"True, but you only had a fifty-year-old photo of a little girl when we started hunting for your lost family members. How is this different?"

Jessica unwound her petite legs. "She has a point. But just because my dad was innocent of the crime he'd been jailed for doesn't mean this Manuel Andersen is . . . or was."

Shannon placed her hands to the small of her back and stretched. "True. All we know is when he was born, that he joined the Navy in 1975 in Jacksonville, Florida, and then was a suspect in a crime in 1988."

"NAS in Orange Park, actually, just south of there." Bailey showed them the map on her phone.

"NAS?" Jessica scrunched her button nose.

"Naval Air Station. See?" She angled the small screen so they could both peer into it. "We can search the enlistment records online. I discovered the website while doing genealogy searches. My uncle was in the Navy, remember?"

"Oh, yeah. Of course." Shannon's hope raised a notch. "I'm getting my laptop." She scooted away from the coffee table and stood.

"I'll go get mine as well." Bailey rose and fished her apartment key from her jeans pocket. She lived just down the way in the same complex.

Jessica's rosebud lips formed a pout. "I need to head back to Tulsa in the morning, but is there something Grady and I can do?"

Shannon reached down to hug her shoulders. "Let's see what we find tonight. Then I'll have a better idea. But I'm guessing we will need Chase or Grady's assistance in looking up his criminal records if Manuel Andersen was ever caught and convicted for that convenience store robbery."

"And the murder of the clerk." Bailey scrunched her mouth to one side before opening the front door. "Back in a sec."

Shannon brought in her laptop and plugged it into her battery saver. "Okay, Jess. I've opened it with my password. You see if you can find anything more about the robbery in 1988 in Fort Meyers. Here is the newspaper's name." She slid one copy to her friend. "I'll do a search on my phone for his name and see if I get any hits."

Jessica scooted closer to the coffee table. "On it."

Bailey returned, plopped on the couch with her laptop balanced on her lap, and began searching naval records.

Shannon watched her friends' intent expressions in the

soft glow of the computer screens. How many hours over the past two years had they spent like this? A warmth spread through her like hot chocolate down her throat on a cold day. "I love y'all."

The two raised their gaze with puzzled expressions. Bailey shrugged. "Back at ya, girlfriend."

A few minutes later Jessica squeaked. "Oh, found something." She sat straighter as if proud she had been the first to contribute. "Listen to this. It's from four days later."

Shannon and Bailey raised their attention from their own screens. Jessica eyed them both then began to read.

"Police located two men of interest in the recent homicide and robbery of the 7-11 on Cleveland Road the evening of July 18, 1988. They were huddled in an abandoned warehouse. After a few rounds of fire, the suspects surrendered. Manuel Andersen and Freddie Ortiz are being arraigned for armed robbery and resisting arrest. At this time, police are not saying if either man will be charged with the murder of Joaquin Guerra, the forty-two-year-old store clerk who leaves behind a wife and five children. Guerra died of his injuries after being rushed to Lee Memorial Hospital. His funeral was held today but none of the relatives were available for comment."

"Great job. Bookmark it." Shannon jotted down the sparse details. "I have found six hits for Manuel Andersen. I'm sorting through them, but so far no one is the correct age."

"If you find one, let me know. I still have a subscription to that find your lost relatives site." Bailey winked. "So far, I've found five Manuel, Manny, or Manfred Andersens enlisted in the Navy during the 1970s."

"That many?" Shannon reared back, resting her weight on her hands behind her.

"Well," Bailey repositioned her laptop. "It was still the Vietnam era, right? Tons of men went to war then."

"Barely. It ended in April of 1975. Manny turned 18 in January, according to the birth certificate you showed us, so I doubt he'd been deployed by then." Jessica's face gleamed.

"Whoa, look who's Miss Wikipedia!" Shannon chuckled.

"I do learn a bit here and there in my freelance research, y'all." Jessica shrugged.

Bailey dipped her finger to her tongue, then swiped it in the air twice. "Score two for Jess."

They all laughed.

Bailey pointed to her screen. "So far, they all were honorably discharged by 1985, but I'm still matching birthdates. I'm betting ours wasn't a career man."

"Hey, Shan. What if we do locate him?" Jessica cocked her head to the side.

"Jayden unloads tomorrow in Orlando, picks up a

short run to Tallahassee, and then has two days before he has a haul for Jackson, Mississippi. Maybe he could track Manny down and speak with him. If he is still alive and living in Florida, that is."

"I hope he's not in the pen." Jessica's eyes rounded.

"Right." Shannon nodded. "Or in a potter's field. They still execute in Florida. But, this morning I found a website listing all the prisoners executed since 1972, and he wasn't listed."

"Slow day for pets and plants?" Jessica raised a blond eyebrow.

"Cold snap made people cancel their spring break plans, I guess." Shannon shrugged. "Frankly, I'm glad neither me nor my staff had to walk dogs today. Brrr."

"If Jayden only has a few days, we need to find something tonight." Bailey ducked her head back to the screen in front of her.

Jessica and Shannon did as well.

After a half-hour, Jessica gasped again. "Found some more."

"What is it?"

"You can stop searching prison records. It took a while, but I found it. It is in the police report from the newspaper dated August 2, 1988." She tapped her screen. "Manuel Andersen has been released from custody following his cooperation in revealing information regarding the convenience store robbery, which resulted in the murder of Joaquin Guerra."

Shannon slapped her hand to her chest. "Well, what do you know. We aren't investigating a murderer after all. That's a relief. Mrs. Perkins will be thrilled."

Her friends let out a sigh at the same time.

"So why haven't I had much luck locating anyone by that name that is in his early 60's?" Shannon glanced a each of her friends, whose expressions appeared as clueless as she felt.

Bailey set her computer aside. "What if he went into witness protection?"

The blood rushed to Shannon's feet. "Oh, girl. Don't go there. Please."

Chapter Four

Wednesday morning, Shannon decided to go see Mrs. Perkins—not only to let her know her nephew was not a murderer after all but to also pump her for more of her life story. Anything she could recall might be a clue that could lead to his whereabouts.

But as Shannon brushed her teeth, her phone barked. That meant her assistant, Tabitha, called. Shannon's eyes flicked to the digital clock sitting on her bathroom countertop. 7:06 a.m. Couldn't be good news.

"Hey, girl. What's . . ."

A frantic soprano voice sounded on the other end. "I went to Mrs. Maple's house and found Chloe on the kitchen floor breathing heavily. Foam is around her mouth. I'm taking her to the emergency vet's on Broadway now." The sound of cars swooshing made her talk more loudly over her Bluetooth. "I'm two blocks away."

Shannon's heart jolted. Mrs. Maple had saved up her pennies to go on a bucket list Caribbean cruise for ten days, leaving Chloe, her sixteen-year-old cat, in the capable hands of Pampered Pets and Plants. "Good thinking. Keep me posted. I'll go by the Liles' and check on their dogs then head over to the Porters' house to feed the hamster and the parrot. Who else needs attention?"

"I fed the Garcias' bulldog last night. And gave him water. But he needs to be walked. If he does his business promptly, they give him two milk bones. They live in the condos in Olmos Park. Poop bags are on top of the dryer in the utility room."

Shannon tucked the phone under her chin and called up the info on her tablet. "Got it." Mrs. Perkins would have to wait. "I'll take care of . . ."

"I'm pulling into the vet's office now. Bye." She clicked off.

Shannon stared at the phone screen. Okay. Bye.

A half-hour later, her cell phone chimed as she unhooked the leash of the bulldog, lovingly named Snorty. "Hey, Bailey. What's . . ."

"I was thinking."

Why did everyone interrupt her sentences today? "About?"

"If I was a middle-aged man whose name had been plastered all over the local papers involving a robbery-homicide at a convenience store, I'd relocate as fast as I could. People only recall the bad stuff, not that he wasn't convicted."

Shannon hoisted herself on the kitchen counter and watched Snorty lap the water from his bowl in between grunts and loud gurgled breaths. Well-named animal. "Assuming he had no wife, kids, or a job."

"Maybe he did, and they went with him. Anyway, why don't I come over again tonight after choir practice and we can expand our search around Florida."

"Sounds great." Her phone buzzed in her ear. She glanced at the screen. "I gotta run. Tabs calling in. We have a sick cat."

"Ugh. Prayers." Bailey clicked off.

Tabs let her know the beast somehow ate a fizzy antacid she'd probably discovered on the floor of the bathroom but would be all right. Shannon rolled her eyes. "Use the credit card and don't tell me how much it is right now. We will settle later with the owner. Let me think about how much of the cost we should absorb . . . no pun intended."

She locked up Snorty and drove to the office. There she did a wider search, this time looking for any Andersens in southern Florida. Wow. She scrolled through four pages, but none listed a phone number or street address, only names, ages, and cities. This would take a while. She decided to concentrate on women around Manny's age and then others who would be twenty or so years younger, perhaps his children. That narrowed it down a bit, but it would still take hours. She had a business to run for goodness sake, and the premature cold snap had moved on, raising the temperature back up to the seventies by this afternoon.

She dialed Jayden's cell.

He answered on the third ring, yelling over the highway noise. "Hey, sweet girl."

"Hey, hon. How's it going?"

"I'm crossing the Alabama-Florida line now. Have three stops to make before I hit Miami. How is the research going?"

"Well, that's why I am calling."

"And I thought you missed my baritone smooth voice."

By his tone, she knew he played with her. She chuckled. "I do, hon. More than you know. Can you do me a favor?"

"Shoot. I'm listening." A sound of an air horn blared. "Sorry. Some idiot in a minivan cut right in front of me. Go ahead."

"When you stop for a break, take a picture of the Andersens in the phonebook and text it to me. Then I can look them up on Bailey's genealogy search."

"Do they still make those things?"

"The searches? Yes. They're still a big craze."

"No, I mean phone books."

"Yeah. They do, though I read an article that says they probably will stop printing the yellow pages within the year."

"Do we still get them?"

"Yes. You never see them because I toss them in the recycling bin." *And because you're never around.*

"Then I'll check at the truck stops. They might have them."

"If the truck stops don't have any, perhaps the libraries would have them."

"Okay . . ." More highway noise blared into her ear, muting his words.

"I can't hear you, Jay."

His voice raised. "I guess this means Manny is not in prison after all?"

"Yep. Jessica found a news article saying the police released him several days later. But I can't locate him in the Fort Meyers area."

"You think he relocated somewhere else in the state?"

"It's worth a try. Bailey said it would make sense for him to move away and start over fresh. I'll keep searching online, too, to see if I can narrow down the cities he may have transferred to."

"If he stayed in Florida. It's a big country, you know. And more and more people are choosing to be ex-pats in the Caribbean and Mexico."

She didn't need to be reminded of how futile this search could turn out. "I gotta to go with my gut. I think he may still be in his home state. Can you check out the phone books?"

"Will do, babe. Love ya."

Hearing him say it sent hot prickles up her arms. Her heart stretched to encase them as they spread to her chest. "And I love you, ox-man."

"What?"

"That's what Mrs. Perkins called you."

His deep laugh tickled her eardrums as he hung up.

That evening, Shannon drove to the hospice facility to check on Mrs. Perkins. Entering the place of near-death sent a quick shiver down her spine. She knew these folks were being taken care of in a dignified and empathetic manner, but it still saddened her. As she walked by each room, she prayed they all knew Jesus and that this was not the end for them, only the beginning.

Standing at room number 14, she tapped on the

partially ajar door. "Mrs. Perkins?"

A weak voice responded. "Yes?"

"It's Shannon Johnson. I have some good news."

"Come in." The voice raised in strength. "You found him already?"

She dashed her gaze to the floor. "No, ma'am. But we did find out he was released four days after that robbery. He didn't kill that clerk."

Relief reduced the wrinkles on the old woman's brow. "Well, praise God for that."

Shannon shuffled over to the bed. "Yes, ma'am." Her hands felt empty. She should have brought flowers. Something to brighten the room.

The soft mechanical whir of the IV machine and whoosh of the air conditioning unit blanketed the raspy breaths of her mentor until she drew closer. It jolted Shannon's senses. Had she gone downhill this quickly? She'd barely been there twenty-four hours.

"Are you okay?"

The old woman smiled weakly. "Considering . . ."

Shannon felt her cheeks warm, then grow cold. "Yes, well . . . may I sit and talk with you for a while?"

Mrs. Perkins nodded and pushed the up button on her bed panel, lifting her head several degrees.

Shannon scooted a wooden chair, much like the ones in the cafeteria of her old high school, closer to the woman's bedside. "Tell me. When did you leave Florida?"

Mrs. Perkins' eyes drifted to another time and place. "1977. Just before Christmas. My sister lived in San Antonio. Her husband was retired army, so they'd settled there near Fort Sam Houston. He passed of cancer that year. I'd lost all attempts to connect with Manny. I had an APO address, but my letters came back unopened. She suggested we move in together." Her feeble shoulders raised to her ears. "I needed a change of scenery. Too many sad memories in Cape Coral."

"Across the way from Fort Meyers, right?"

"That's correct. You have been researching." She waggled her bony finger at Shannon's face.

"So have Bailey and Jessica."

"You think he still lives in Florida, then?"

"Maybe. We haven't had much luck finding him in the Fort Meyers area." Shannon shrugged. "Jayden is checking phone book directories at truck stops between Tallahassee and Miami, but we are going to keep searching the internet."

The woman clucked, "My, so much information is public knowledge these days."

"Yes, it is. Kinda scary, but also helpful. Anyway, I wanted you to know he wasn't in prison . . ." She stopped before "or executed" slid off her tongue.

A smile curled the crinkled lips. They seemed so much

paler today. Shannon wondered if the nurses would give her an update on Mrs. Perkins's condition. Probably not. It wasn't as if Shannon could pass for her granddaughter. That would be lying anyway.

As if reading her mind, Mrs. Perkins motioned for her to scoot a tad closer. "I signed papers allowing you to speak to my doctors. Mr. Albert Jordan is my attorney. Do you know him from church? With my sister deceased for the past two years, he has changed my will to make you executor."

"Me?" Shannon felt the room ripple. Maybe it was her heart instead. Tornadoes plagued Texas but not very many earthquakes.

"I don't have much that hasn't already been given away, but I do have a few bonds and such. And some jewelry in a safety deposit box. He has the key. Sell it for what you can. I want ninety percent to go to the church remodeling fund."

She didn't want to talk of death, but the woman's life. "Mrs. Perkins, I . . ."

"Now, dear. I told you I have no kin. My other sister and her husband could never have children. They're both gone now, of course. And I never remarried after mine died in 'Nam. Manny is the only living relative I may have, and we haven't spoken since 1975."

"I know." Shannon glanced at her hands. So sad how

families drifted apart. She'd seen the reunion of Bailey's family after five decades of hurt and anger were dispelled. Could she really do the same for Mrs. Perkins and her nephew?

Mrs. Perkins cleared her throat. "I had a long talk with the Lord. Your name kept popping into my brain. I believe He wants me to give the remaining ten percent to you and Jayden."

Shannon's mouth opened as she gazed into her mentor's clouded eyes. Had she heard correctly?

"I don't know what He plans for you to do with it, but there it is. I'm confident He wants you to have it."

Tears gathered in the corners of Shannon's eyes. Her tongue felt foreign in her mouth. "I . . . I don't know what to say. Th . . . thank you."

Mrs. Perkins turned her head to the window. Outside a maple tree branch swayed, its new spring leaves trying to bud despite the chilly north winds that had recently whistled through. It reminded Shannon of this dear woman in her last days striving to remain positive and upbeat.

"I need to rest now." Her voice sounded weaker.

Shannon brushed the woman's cheek with the back of her hand. "Of course. You take care. I'll visit again soon."

Mrs. Perkins responded with a slight nod as her eyes closed and her raspy breathing deepened.

Shannon tip-toed from the room. In the corridor, she

spotted a nurse. "May I speak with you about Mrs. Grace Perkins? I'm Shannon Johnson."

Recognition showed on the medical attendant's face. "Yes, how do you do? Would you mind showing me some identification, first? Protocol."

"Of course not." Shannon dug into her purse and pulled out her wallet. She opened it to reveal her driver's license. "Here you are . . ." she glanced at the name tag. "Ms. Salvador." Hm, the woman's name meant "one who saves" in Spanish. Nice.

The nurse studied it for a moment. "Thank you, Shannon. What can I help you with?"

"Is she . . . fading?"

"We are keeping her comfortable. The pain can get pretty intense with this type of cancer."

"Which is . . ."

The nurse blinked as if surprised Shannon didn't know. "Pancreatic. Stage 4."

"Meaning?"

"It's spread throughout her body." Her face softened. "Nothing can be done at this point except to keep her pain level as low as possible. Most of the time she will be floating in and out of the fog of heavy medication. I'm so sorry."

Shannon gulped in response to the warm expression in the attendant's eyes. The woman dealt with death daily but hadn't been hardened by it. Empathy still hung in her voice.

"Bless you for all you are doing for her." Shannon scanned the hallway. "And everyone else here. It is quite a calling."

The woman's eyes lowered toward the small cross around Shannon's neck. "Knowing I am sending them home helps. I silently pray over each and every soul here that they will find rest in the arms of our Lord."

Shannon winked. "I know He hears your prayers. Mrs. Perkins says since He is the Way, He never gives up on showing anyone and everyone that. He doesn't want anyone to perish."

She whispered into Shannon's ear with a return wink. "Amen."

A chime sounded throughout the hallway. "Oops. Duty calls." She shuffled off to answer the beeping sound in room eleven.

Chapter Five

As Shannon walked down the corridor to the exit, a blur of scrubs dashed past her in the opposite direction. She turned back to see medical personnel rushing to room eleven, one with a crash cart. The room Ms. Salvador had gone to investigate.

The finality of life punched her in the gut. This was a hospice facility, after all. No one left here alive. Sooner than Shannon wanted, it might be Mrs. Perkins they rushed to assist.

A renewed urgency to find Manny Andersen swelled in her heart. She sent up a quick prayer for whoever in that room hung onto this life by a thread. She pushed open the double doors to the sunlit lobby filled with cheery colored furniture nested amongst evergreen potted plants. What a contrast.

Though the temperatures had risen back into the

comfortable seventies, she drew her sweater closer and, with her head down, shuffled through the grass to the parking lot. Once inside her car and buckled in, she punched Jayden's number.

"Hey, girl. Three calls in a week. You okay?"

"I'm at the hospice place. I think one of the patients just died."

The whirr of highway noise filtered through her speakerphone. But no soothing male voice.

"Jayden?"

"I'm here. Just sorry I'm not there."

His tone hugged her tight, even hundreds of miles away. "I know. But I had a good talk with Mrs. Perkins. Seems after Manny left, and it sunk in that he wouldn't be returning, her widowed sister persuaded her to move to San Antonio in 1977. But that's not all she told me."

"Go on . . ."

"She's put us in her will, Jay."

"Seriously? Wow." The engine hum increased as he shifted through the gears.

"I doubt she has much. You saw her old place. But the gesture is so kind. I want to bring her flowers. A really nice bouquet to brighten her room."

"Do it. She had fake daisies in a planter out front of her apartment. I spotted them the day we moved her out. Maybe they are her favorite."

Shannon smiled. Her hubby noticed things many men didn't. "Good thinking, hon. I'll do that. Thanks."

"Oh, I didn't send you a shot of the phone book in Tallahassee because the Andersens in it were all one family living at the same address and none of them were a Manuel or a Manny."

"Okay. But you realize he'd be in his sixties now, so he could have had kids, even grandkids."

Silence. Then a soft huff. "Oh. Right. Sorry."

"Not a big deal. You can catch it on the flip side."

His laughter blasted into her ear. "Picking up the trucking lingo for the return trip, are we? Well, 10-4 backdoor. Love ya, hon. Better git. The traffic is getting kinda thick. Must be a wreck up ahead."

She heard the grinding of the down gears. "Stay safe. Love ya, hon."

She disconnected the call and stared at the screen for a minute. Her heart swelled with joy and ached with loneliness at the same time.

How did military wives handle it? Had Manny married? Tonight, she definitely had to surf the web some more. But where to begin?

A thought pushed to the front of her mind. She recalled the advice Bailey's sister-in-law had given Bailey when she began searching for her long-lost relatives. Start with wedding announcements and obituaries, they often list family members.

Shannon slapped the steering wheel. "Thank you, Lord. I'll do just that. After work, that is." She pulled out of the parking lot and headed toward Terrell Hills to walk and feed the Liebermans' two poodles, Salt and Pepper.

That night, as she crunched her salad, an envelope appeared at the bottom right of her laptop screen. She minimized the wedding announcements from the *Jacksonville Florida Times Union* from 1975 and pulled up the email. It was from Jayden.

"I stopped off at the library in Orlando and found they had phone books from all the major cities in Florida. Here are all the Andersens in Orlando, Miami, Miami Beach, Jacksonville, Tallahassee, Boca Raton, and Fort Meyers. That ought to keep you off the streets. (Smiley winking face emoji). Dinner break over. Back on the road. Call you from Miami tomorrow."

She grinned. What a guy. She clicked on the attachments and found twelve photocopied pages. Holy Moley. She saved them, then began to divvy them up into three different documents. Then she forwarded one to Jessica and one to Bailey with a text message.

Hey, Jayden's been busy. Here are phonebook pages of Andersens in Florida. Can you begin to call and ask if they know of a Manuel? Go ahead and tell them his aunt is dying, and we are trying to locate him. Thanks.

Within a few minutes, she got okay emojis from both of her friends. She pulled up the first page of her assigned numbers, grabbed her phone, and began to dial. It was 6:12 p.m. Florida was an hour ahead. Shouldn't be too late to bug people she didn't know.

She gave up for the night at 7:55 p.m., her time. Growing up, her household rule had been to never contact anyone after nine at night. Shannon clung to that social protocol even though folks had do-not-disturb modes and voice mail now.

Most of the people she spoke with had been kind and understanding, but none of them knew anyone named Manuel Andersen. Well, so much for the Jacksonville area down to Orlando. Except for the seven that hadn't answered. She'd left a detailed voice message at those households. She stretched and closed the lid to her laptop. Time to veg out on her favorite crime investigation show anyway.

Shannon nuked some herbal tea, curled up on the couch, and flicked the remote control. Halfway through the show she slumped to a fetal position and pulled the crocheted afghan, made by her great aunt, up to her knees.

Within minutes, she fell asleep without learning who had shot the banker's daughter.

A beep from her phone filtered into her dreams. Then a female voice. She blinked and reached through the cobwebs of her brain to realize someone left a message on her phone. She bolted upright, grabbed her cell, and swiped the screen. 10:12 p.m. She tapped the icon for the voicemail messages. One from 10:11 p.m. It had been real. She punched in her passcode and turned up the volume.

"Hi. My name is Beverley Andersen. I'm married to Parker Andersen. I hope I'm not calling too late. My husband's dad was named Manuel, but he hasn't had contact with him in years. Last he heard, his dad moved to Tallahassee after the divorce when Parker was thirteen. That would have been in 1989, I think. His wife, Parker's mom, is Martha Walters now. She remarried fifteen years ago. Her number is 904-625-9941. She lives in Midlothian about thirty minutes south of Jacksonville, where we live. Hope that helps."

Shannon saved the voice mail, hugged her phone to her chest, and sent a thank you to the ceiling.

Chapter Six

Bailey stood outside her apartment complex watching for the familiar red sports car. Chase pulled up a few minutes later. He slowed to a stop and let down the window. "Hey, good looking. Need a ride?"

She chuckled and walked to the passenger side. Before her hand touched the door latch, his warm fingers encircled it. She jumped. When did he get out of the car?

"Don't you dare open that yourself. Let me."

Wedged between his tall frame and the car door, she may have felt trapped a year ago. But now a total opposite sensation washed over her. She raised on tip-toe and pecked his cheek before sliding into the bucket seat.

The grin on his face deepened, which made her blush. She took in a breath to calm her senses. *Take it slow, girl. Don't let your heart race ahead of your head.*

As he slipped into the driver's seat, he leaned in to

brush her lips with his. "Breakfast first or go see Mrs. Perkins?"

"Breakfast. It may still be too early."

Chase pressed the pedal to accelerate. The engine roused from a soft purr to a roar. Bailey pictured half the curtained windows in her complex fluttering as annoyed residents peered out. "Shhh. Chase. It's only seven."

"Time for everyone to get up and out to greet the day, then. They'll thank me later."

She laughed. Breakfast dates with this guy highlighted her week. With his erratic schedule as a detective, early morning was the least interrupted time for him. Plus, he always arrived freshly showered, shaved, and newly splashed with cologne. She'd come to cherish these moments.

Shannon must have checked her bedside clock at least six times during the night. At 6:45 a.m., she figured it might be safe to call. At least she hoped so. Most elderly people rose early, right? Maybe Mrs. Walters would be eating breakfast or something at a quarter to eight.

Stifling a yawn as she poured herself a second cup of coffee, Shannon inhaled a deep, long breath to steady her nerves, exhaled it with a silent prayer, and dialed the number. A woman answered on the third ring.

"Hello? If this is a solicitation call, I'm hanging up now."

Shannon waved her hand out in front of her as if the person she called could see her. "No, ma'am. It is not, and I hope I'm not calling too early in the morning. Is this a good time to speak to Martha Walters?"

"I'm Martha Walters." A question of "who is this?" hung in her answer.

"Oh, good. Okay, this is going to sound bizarre but please hear me out. It's not a prank or anything like that. I don't want money and I'm not selling anything. My name is Shannon and your daughter-in-law, Beverley, gave me your phone number last night."

"I see."

Shannon knew by the tone of her voice she really didn't.

"I am calling for a dear friend, Mrs. Grace Perkins, who is dying."

She heard a chair leg screeching across the floor. Rustling came over the phone, but no voice. Then the woman responded as if out of breath. "Manny's aunt. From Texas?"

Shannon's system jolted. She'd definitely found the right person. "Yes, yes. Exactly. I know you have been divorced a long time . . ."

"Yes, we have." A residual bitterness coated her reply.

"I don't suppose you'd know . . ."

"Where he is?" She let off a harsh scoff. "No, and frankly, I don't care. If he is still alive, and I doubt it, check the homeless shelters and rehab hospitals. Maybe the jails. I left him for a reason."

Wow. The resentment hadn't faded much with time. "Thanks, I will. May I ask how you knew Mrs. Perkins had moved to Texas?"

"You may as well know. Back when I was young and stupid . . ." Another scoff. "I tried to get Manny and her back together. But he wouldn't budge. Always had a stubborn streak."

"Mrs. Perkins told me he left in a huff at eighteen and she never heard from him again."

"Well, that's sort of true."

Shannon scrunched her eyebrows. "Can you tell me about that?"

"I guess." She heard the woman sigh through the phone. "We met in 1976 when he was in the Navy on shore leave. Married three months later before he deployed to the Middle East when things heated up there again. Got pregnant on our honeymoon, so I found her address amongst his things and sent her a letter. It came back with a forwarding address in San Antonio, Texas. I kept it, and when Parker was born, I sent her a photo of him. I got a very nice thank-you note, and a booklet from a savings account in Fort Meyers she opened for him with $250 in it. I never told Manny, but when Parker turned twenty-one, we drove back to Fort Meyers together and got the money. Seems she'd deposited ten dollars a month into the account all that time, and on his birthday each year she added another fifty dollars. With interest, it equaled close to $4,000. In 1998, that was enough for him to put a down payment on a reliable car."

Shannon slammed her spine into her dinette chair. Why hadn't Mrs. Perkins told her any of this? It would surely have saved time. She rubbed her forehead. "Thanks, Martha. I greatly appreciate your time and information. But you have no idea . . ."

"Not in the least. Look, when he came back stateside, Manny had changed. He became moody with a hair-trigger temper. Drank a lot, too. Eventually, the Navy quietly shoved him out the door, though he did discharge honorably. Had trouble holding a job in the real world. I put up with it and worked to keep us afloat. But when he got tangled up in that convenience store robbery, that's when I packed up with Parker and moved back to Jacksonville to my parent's house.

"After the cops released him, he tracked us down and pleaded with me to come back. His breath could have started a distillery. My dad kicked him out and helped me file for a divorce. Never got much alimony or child support. Each time Manny got a job, they'd glean his salary, but he never stayed employed very long. When Parker turned fifteen, the checks stopped coming. He surfaced in a Tallahassee hospital suffering from malnutrition and exposure four years later. Drugs, I think. The social worker got ahold of my parents. Manny had listed me as next of kin at that last known address."

Shannon calculated the timeline in her head, writing down the dates on the back of her utility bill envelope, the closest thing to paper she could grab and stay on the line. "So that would have been in 1996? Twenty-three years ago? Two years before you and Parker went to Fort Meyers."

"Sounds about right." Martha's tone went flat.

Twenty-three years sounded like forever ago to Shannon, who was only thirty-one. Who knew where Manuel Andersen would be now? Maybe in a potter's field after all.

She heard Martha sigh through the receiver. "Look, I have to go. My husband needs to go to the eye doctor."

"Oh, yes. Sure. Listen, thank you so very much. I really appreciate your time. Sorry to dredge up bad memories."

The woman's voice mellowed. "Listen, tell Mrs.

Perkins thanks for the money she put in that account for Parker all those years. She must be a very sweet person. I'm sorry she isn't long for this earth."

With that, Martha Walters ended the call.

Shannon sat at the table tapping her pen. Where did she go from here? Were hospital records public knowledge? No, probably not. Privacy laws and all that. But someone had to have picked him up and taken him there. The police? Could she access their records? Maybe Chase could help since he was the county sheriff's chief detective now.

She texted Bailey to call her as soon as she could. She knew she'd be seeing Chase for one of their breakfast dates this morning.

One thing for sure, she needed to start her search in Tallahassee, Manny's last known location. And, Jayden would be headed back that way in two days. He'd have a forty-eight-hour layover before loading up and heading to Jackson, Mississippi.

Shannon sat up straight. Hey. She could meet him there. Could they afford for her to fly, or should she drive it? She did a mileage search. Sheesh, it was a long way! She'd be on the road more than twelve hours straight. Airfare? She pulled up a cheap flight site. Oh, no way. Not cheap enough.

Maybe take a bus? That would be safer than driving

by herself cross-country. She checked the fare prices and then logged onto their savings account. Busing would work. They could easily afford it. She texted Jayden to call her when he got a break and headed out the door to the office.

Viewing the schedule on her calendar app, she smiled as she scanned the upcoming pet and plant care appointments. Perfect timing. Tabitha could handle things for a few days. The Liebermann family and the Porters had returned yesterday, and Mrs. Maple had been reunited with her fluffy Chloe who now had a voracious appetite. The Garcia family would return tomorrow to their beloved, slobbering bulldog. That left only three customers until the twenty-fifth when they picked up four more over the weekend.

Yes, very doable. She deserved a small break anyway. She hadn't had one since she and Bailey went to Oklahoma with Jessica almost a year ago.

Jayden called her about ten-thirty. "Hey, girl. Got your message."

"You miss me?"

"Um, yeah. Sure, I do. But why do you ask?"

"What if I was there in Tallahassee waiting for you tomorrow?"

Jayden's deep laugh fluttered into her heart. "It's too early for Santa Claus, and I don't believe in the tooth fairy, so . . .”

She popped tension from her neck and switched the phone to the other ear. “I'm serious. I think I found Manny, or at least where he was twenty-three years ago.”

“In Tallahassee? Babe, I sent you that phone book. No Andersens named Manuel or Manny in it.”

“I know. He may not have a phone. Besides everyone has cells now, so a lot of people don't even bother with landlines. All I know is I got in touch with his ex-wife, and she said the last she heard he was hospitalized there and . . .” She realized she hadn't taken a breath.

“Whoa . . . slow down. Start from the beginning.”

She did.

“Okay, girl. I don't want you running around homeless shelters and drunk tanks on your own. How are you getting here?”

“Bus. I can leave today and get there by noon tomorrow. We have the money.”

“Great. Book us a motel room and text me the location. I'll meet you there. But hon?”

“Yeah?”

“Be careful. I love you.”

“I love ya back. And more. See you soon. I'll pack the black nightgown.”

He playfully groaned. “Girl, you are messin' with my mind now.”

With a giggle, she hung up. She danced around the office like a pre-teen in love. That's when she saw Tabitha standing at the entrance laughing at her.

"Heard from Jayden, huh?"

"Yep. And you better sit down because I am heading out of town in two hours." Shannon motioned to the chair next to the desk.

After hearing the shortened version, Tabitha shooed Shannon out the door reassuring her she had everything handled.

She packed a bag and dashed to the hospice to let Mrs. Perkins know her plans—and to give her Martha Walter's message.

Mrs. Perkins sat upright in bed, but her eyes didn't appear very bright.

Shannon tiptoed over to her beside. "Hey, are you all right?"

The old woman reached out a shaky hand. "The Lord answers again. I needed a prayer partner and here you are."

Worry gripped Shannon's heart as she pulled over the chair. "I'll pray with you, of course. Tell me why."

"Two. They've lost two here in the past day."

Shannon tilted her head and stroked the woman's palm. "Oh, dear. I am sorry." She bit her tongue before it spouted out to her mentor that this was the place people came to die . . . like her. Perhaps the reality of it had finally sunk into the woman's still sharp mind.

"Nurses say they were both believers, so they are home. That's a blessing, still . . ."

Shannon scooted closer. "Let's pray, and then I have some good news to tell you." She winked and then bowed her head.

By the time she left, Mrs. Perkin's eyes held a slight twinkle again.

Halfway to the bus station, Shannon realized she'd forgotten to contact Bailey or Jessica. Neither had returned her texts. Maybe they figured they'd talk at choir practice. Bailey might be on her lunch break. Jessica, back in Tulsa, could be having lunch with Grady. She texted Jess to tell her to call her when she got a chance and then told her Bluetooth to call Bailey.

Bailey listened. "Wow, this is so cool. It's got to be a God thing that Jayden is there right now, too."

"For sure. Listen I don't have long because I am headed to the bus station now. Can you check on Mrs. P. tomorrow? They've lost two in the past day or so, and I think that fact has hit her pretty hard."

"I know. Chase and I went to see her this morning. Did she tell you about someone being in her room?"

"No. What do you mean?"

"Chase calmed her down by telling her the nurses were probably assigned to check on them several times a night.

He said that is what they did when his grandmother was in a nursing home."

Something jerked Shannon's heart. *Good explanation, and probable. Right?* The place seemed secure, and Mrs. Perkins said her jewelry lay in a safety deposit box. Still . . ."Do you think someone like an orderly could be pilfering people's rooms?"

"Nah, I think she is on edge. Understandably. Chase talked to the coroner and he said sometimes the pain meds they give hospice patients can make them a bit hallucinogenic. We'll keep an eye on her. Listen, have a great time with Jayden and keep me posted on what happens."

"Girl, we are great friends, but some things I don't share." Shannon chuckled.

"Ew. Stop. No. I meant on the Manny investigation."

"I know. But you did walk into that one."

Bailey's melodic laugh came through. "I did, didn't I? Take care. Stay safe."

Shannon hung up and frowned. Stay safe? That's what Jayden had said as well.

Weird.

She sloughed off a chill scooting up her neck, parked the car, and headed inside the bus station, dragging her wheeled suitcase behind her.

Chapter Seven

The bus swelled with passengers. One vacant seat remained, next to a man. Great. She hoped he didn't want to chat nonstop for the next twenty-three hours. Or hit on her.

At least he had taken the window seat, so she didn't have to crawl over him. The chatter of the other folks settling in for the ride made normal conversation impossible, so she pointed to the blue striped upholstery next to him.

He nodded with a sweep of his hand, indicating its availability. With a head bob and a quick grin, she took her seat. He extended his hand. "Matt." His voice barely carried over the thirty-odd conversations going on at the same time—and a crying baby, and an older man with a hacking, gurgled cough. *Thank you, Lord, I am not seated next to him.*

She took his hand in a firm shake. "Shannon. Going to Tallahassee to meet my *husband*, who is on business there." May as well establish that fact right off the bat.

Matt didn't flinch. But his eyes warmed as he leaned toward her ear. "Lucky man, if you don't mind me saying so."

"Not at all, but I'm the lucky one. More like blessed."

"Amen."

So, he was a believer. Good. She relaxed a bit. Especially when she noticed a wedding band on his hand.

Her traveling companion's breath whiffed of a recently devoured breath mint. It made Shannon a bit self-conscious. She reached in her purse for a stick of sugarless peppermint gum.

"And you?" She raised an eyebrow as she folded the gum in thirds and placed it in her mouth.

"Headed for Pensacola. Though I've been to Tallahassee many times on business myself. Beautiful city. Very lush and green there with tall trees. Like the whole city is nestled in a giant park."

"Sounds lovely."

The bus driver boarded, swished the doors closed, and started up the engine. Immediately, as if on cue, the din of voices calmed down.

"Next stop Houston, Beaumont, Lake Charles, Lafayette, Baton Rouge, New Orleans, Slidell, Gulf Port,

Mobile, Pensacola, Panama City, Tallahassee. If you are not going to any of them, you're on the wrong bus, folks."

Chuckles filtered through the cabin.

He peered in his rearview mirror, saw no one start to disembark, and shrugged. "Off we go then." The airbrakes released with a hiss as the low rumble of the engine vibrated the floor.

Matt gazed out the window as they left the downtown San Antonio terminal and wove through the narrow streets toward the highway. Shannon peered over his shoulder, saying goodbye to her hometown, almost swallowed by the booming metropolis. Once they had maneuvered through the traffic and entered onto I-10, Matt turned his face back to her.

"How long are you staying there?"

"Only a few days. Why?"

"Oh, I'd write down some sites for you. They have several antebellum mansions there to tour and an excellent state museum. And if you are a nature nut, head for the Alfred Maclay State Park or Lake Jackson Mounds."

"Thanks."

He shifted toward her, but in a non-threatening way. His head pointed to the space between the bucket seats as his lips curled in a smirk. The man behind them had already begun to snore.

Shannon put her hand to her mouth to keep her

laughter inside.

"My son used to do that. Within three blocks, he'd be out like a light." He snapped his fingers. "He always assumed grandma lived just down the street, not two and a half hours away, and wondered why we didn't see her as much. He'd whine, 'I wanna go see gran-ma.'"

His imitation of a small child made Shannon giggle again.

"Finally, one Christmas, my wife kept him awake the whole way. Miserable trip. He either chatted or whined or kicked the back of my seat the whole time." He shook his head. "Never let him live it down either. We tell the story to his kids now."

Getting a better look at him in the sunlight of the highway, Shannon saw the crow's feet around his eyes and a slight peppering of his sideburns. She guessed him to be in his fifties. "We don't have kids yet."

He waggled a finger at her. "Don't wait too long. If the good Lord grants it. Children are a blessing. They hold you accountable and make you a better person."

His honesty jolted her a bit. "How many did you have?"

"Three. All unique, all different. My son lives in Atlanta, one daughter's in Chicago, and the other's in Belgium. She's in international relations."

"You and your wife must miss them."

A cloak of melancholy spread across his face. "Beth went home to the Lord five years ago. Ovarian cancer."

Shannon bit her lip. "I'm so sorry."

He waved it away. "I brought her up in our conversation. You didn't know."

"I have a dear friend in hospice right now with stage four cancer. That's why I'm headed to Tallahassee. To see if I can locate her long-lost kin and let them know."

"I thought you were . . ."

"Yes, my husband is meeting me there. He is taking a few days off to help me search. He travels a lot for work." Why had her tongue loosened with this man? Did he even care? His expression indicated he did.

"You have any clues?"

"Twenty or so years ago, he was hospitalized for exposure and malnutrition in Tallahassee. That's all we know, really, besides his name and birthdate."

"Homeless, then?"

"We think so, but I'm not certain."

Matt clucked his tongue. "He may not be alive now. The average street person lives thirty years less than the rest of us. Drugs, harsh environment, and improper diet play a major factor. And while many hang out all their lives in the same city and form a sort of community, a lot of cities give them a meal, a few bucks, and a one-way bus ticket out of town." He jabbed his finger across the aisle.

Shannon turned her head to view a man with a scraggly beard halfway down his smudged shirt. His face and hands appeared clean, but his tan slacks were torn and stained. Next to him sat a woman with ratted hair and sallow eyes, rocking a small child wrapped in a threadbare shawl.

"Did you know the average age of a homeless person is nine? Most people think they are all old, demented veterans or drug addicts. Not so."

Tears filled her eyes. What a sheltered life she'd lived. She'd always ignored them with their cardboard signs, figuring any money she placed in their palms would soon be in a drug dealer's pocket. Never did she consider they'd have family.

"I fear the man I am looking for may be just that."

"I'm a social worker for the state of Florida. I deal with folks like them all the time. If you need help searching through records, let me know." Matt handed her his business card.

Shannon blinked. Here she had grumbled about sitting next to him and it seems God had orchestrated it. She gave him a head bob and slipped it in her pocket. "Thanks, truly." Then she pulled one of her cards from her wallet. "I can give you his name and date of birth. Oh, and he's a Navy vet. Served from 1975 to 1988, I think. Possibly stationed out of Jacksonville." She cocked her head. "He may have a criminal record, too."

Matt clicked his ballpoint pen and wrote down the information on the back of her card without comment. He then flipped it over. "Pampered Plants and Pets? You own this business?"

She shifted her shoulders back. "I do."

"Huh." He pushed out his lower lip as his eyes scanned the card, then smiled. "Good for you."

Then he reached between his legs and pulled out a black case. Unzipping it, he lifted out a small laptop. The state of Florida seal appeared on the screen. "Let's see what we can find, eh?"

Her eyes widened as he keyed in a passcode to open the site. "This is extremely kind of you."

He shrugged. "May as well pass the time, right? Besides, I have a vested interest in reuniting these people with their families. Most are estranged for some reason or another. Tell me a bit more about Manny."

By the time they pulled into Houston, Matt knew as much as she did. But he didn't have much luck locating Manny's current whereabouts.

"Don't give up hope. There are several other sites we can search. But first, I need to get something to eat and stretch my legs."

The bus pulled into the station, rocked to a halt, and the glass doors whooshed opened. Matt rose with a yawn, hands high over his head. Shannon shifted her knees to let him pass.

As he scooted past her, he halted. "Get you anything?"

She handed him a five-dollar bill. "A coffee, cream no sugar, and some peanut butter crackers."

"Be right back."

She grabbed his sleeve. "Matt. Do you always travel by bus?"

He scoffed. "Heck, no. My rental car broke down while I was at a convention in San Antonio. The agency booked me on this bus back to Pensacola where my office is now. Too cheap for airfare and I didn't want to rent another car from the agency they contract with. Third one in four months that had engine problems." He rolled his eyes and exited.

Okay, then. Guess God really did have this planned out. A new confidence in the possibility of reuniting Mrs. Perkins and Manny Andersen shot through her veins and nestled in her heart.

Chapter Eight

Shannon called Bailey to see about Mrs. Perkins and to tell her about the serendipity of meeting Matt on the bus.

"Wow, that is amazing. What a lead God's plopped into your lap."

"I know, right? How is Mrs. P.?"

Bailey's sigh pressed through the receiver. "I dropped by on the way home from work. Another rough day. They lost another one. To be expected I think, but it is like wiping Mrs. Perkins's nose in it, you know?"

Shannon's whole body ached for her mentor. "Yeah. But maybe there is a peace, too, knowing they are no longer suffering and soon she won't either. Though I sure hate to think of my world without her in it." She sucked in a breath to keep tears from blurring her vision of the bus's interior.

"Good point. Maybe I can find some scripture to cheer her up." Bailey laughed. "Though she probably could quote a ton of them to *me*. Gotta run. Tell Jayden I said, 'Hi.'"

Shannon clicked to end the call and pocketed her phone. Matt sat down beside her and handed her the coffee and crackers. "Bad news?"

"The lady in hospice? My friend went by to check on her and found her a bit down in the dumps. A patient passed on today. That's three so far this week."

His eyes held sympathy. "Well, no one walks out of hospice, you know."

She shrugged and tore open the cellophane wrapping. "Yeah, I get that."

"Then we need to do some more searching. We have a long way to travel so it gives us time. Give me a while to see what I can find."

"Thank you so much. I really appreciate your help."

He nodded as he reopened his laptop.

As the bus pulled out of the station, he began clicking the keys.

Shannon closed her eyes to pray. For his search, for Mrs. Perkins, Jayden's safe travel across Florida, and for all the nurses caring for the people at that center. How hard it would be to watch people die every day. In a few minutes, her brain floated into a soft dream as her chin flopped to her chest.

Matt's voice filtered into her dream. "Aha. I found something."

Her brain recognized reality and yanked her from her deep nap. She rubbed her eyes and sat up straighter. "Huh?"

His cheeks reddened. "Oh, sorry. I didn't realize you were napping. I've been in a research zone, I guess."

A yawn forced its way through her mouth. The sunset filtered through the window, adding a soft hue of golds and pinks to the interior. "That's okay. You said you found something?"

"Yes." He repositioned in his seat in order to share the screen with her. "This is from close to four years ago. He was a resident at a halfway house in Tallahassee for addicts and street people."

She straightened as encouragement lit up her mood like a candle's flicker on a cold, dreary night. "Really? That means he could still live in Tallahassee."

"A good possibility. I know this place, and it's a reputable one. They really help people get back on their feet. They give them a burner phone so potential employers can reach them. Living in the facility gives them a legitimate address to receive mail. They have computers, so the residents can receive emails from job search sites. In the meantime, they earn their keep by doing day jobs or selling baked goods to business offices. They have these places all over the southern part of the United States."

Matt pulled out a small notepad from his briefcase and jotted down the name and address. "My guess is if you go by and speak with the director, explain the situation, and beg for mercy, he might give you information on where Manny is now. If he or she hesitates, have them call me for verification."

Shannon's mind had fully awakened by now. She blinked as if to make sure what he wrote truly existed. "Wow. This is . . . fabulous. Thanks so much, Matt. It would have taken me weeks, if not months, to find this out."

And months she didn't have. Or weeks. The idea of Mrs. Perkins not being on earth much longer hit her afresh. "And by then, it might have been too late."

He shrugged in humility. "Not a big deal. I have resources you don't. Like I said, reuniting these folks with their families makes my blood pump." He ripped off the piece of paper and handed it to her as they pulled into Lake Charles, Louisiana. "Halfway there."

She glanced through the bus's window as several people disembarked. "My turn to stretch my legs."

He gave her a nod and returned his attention to his

laptop.

Shannon eased her long legs into the aisle and rose. She pressed her hand into her lower back and threw her shoulder blades back to ease the ache of sitting for so long. Then she traipsed down the steel rutted steps into Louisiana for the first time in her life, though she'd learned her ancestors had been enslaved there centuries ago. Lush, green, and humid.

She felt hungry but didn't want vending machine food. She wandered toward the street to better view the city as dusk settled in. Maybe there would be a convenience store or a fast-food restaurant close by. As she scanned up and down the street, she saw two men dressed in khaki casual-styled pants and buttoned-down shirts, carrying a basket of pastries.

A sensation whispered over her as if the angels had breathed on her. What were the odds? She waved to them. "How much?"

The men looked both ways and then dashed across the street to her. "Two dollars a loaf, ma'am. We have banana nut bread and cranberry walnut bread."

She dug out four one-dollar bills. "Here. I'll take one of each."

The men grinned and handed her two small, oblong mounds of bread wrapped in cellophane, each with a brightly colored thank you sticker. Then they handed her a paper napkin.

She took the wonderful-smelling baked goods and grinned. "My mouth is watering already. God bless you. I hope you two find good jobs soon."

Both vendors blinked at her knowledge of their plight. The taller one thanked her as a few other passengers from the bus wandered over to see what they had for sale.

As the bus left the station, Shannon couldn't help but snicker. The inside of the cabin filled with the aroma of freshly baked fruit bread as the rustle of plastic wrap filled the air.

Matt winked at her and returned his gaze to his e-book.

Chapter Nine

She knew she shouldn't worry so much. It was nerves or the devil tapping her shoulder. Faith dispelled fear. She needed a boost of it.

Mrs. Perkins squeezed her eyes closed a bit tighter and began reciting a psalm in her head that always brought her peace. She heard the footsteps shuffle closer. This time, she felt a slight tug on her IV line.

Should she pretend to wake up and speak to the intruder? Or lie there and breathe deeply as if still asleep?

Through her eyelids, she detected the movement of a shadow. A small click, like a top popping off, echoed in her right ear. A cold rush entered her veins.

She lost the next verse of the psalm as her mind tumbled down a deep, dark hole. It couldn't be hell? Dear Lord, no. It felt too cold. Besides, she'd made a habit of confessing her sins at the end of each day, and she knew

Jesus was her Redeemer. This sure wasn't how she'd pictured heaven, though.

She must still be on this earth, though her brain couldn't quite grasp reality at the moment. Something swirled her further and further down, carried by a dark rushing sound. Was she drowning? Wouldn't she feel wet if she was?

Her fingernails clawed the sheets, then released as her tightly-held breath left her lungs.

The footsteps faded away in an eerie echo that bounced off the edge of her consciousness.

The soft glow of Shannon's phone screen provided enough light for her to read in the dark cabin of the bus as it traveled across Louisiana toward Mississippi. They passed through New Orleans, but despite the city lights, she couldn't view much of it through the misty rain. By the time they reached the bus station, it was closed for the night. A few souls lingered around the porte-cochere waiting for someone to disembark, or perhaps just hanging out in a drier spot. The homeless family left, carrying the sleeping child. As they passed, she tapped the man's hand and slipped a twenty-dollar bill in it. "I'll be praying for y'all."

His eyes stretched into his eyebrows. "Thanks, ma'am. God bless you."

He showed it to his wife after they reached the sidewalk. She smiled and turned back to the bus windows to wave. Shannon leaned over past Matt to return her gesture as the bus pulled out.

Matt snorted and repositioned himself, then his breaths deepened and slowed again.

Shannon clicked off her phone and snuggled down into her seat, stretching her legs under the one in front of her. May as well get some sleep. Soon the humming of the wheels on the highway pavement and the soft churning of the bus engine helped her drift off.

However, the bus puddle-jumped through town after town. Slidell, Gulfport, Biloxi, Mobile, and a few in between, all with stops of about twenty to thirty minutes. The bus rocking to a halt with its whoosh of air brakes, the bright terminal lights, and the under-storage compartment metal doors slamming jolted her out of her dreamless half-sleep each time. Worse than being in the hospital.

At Biloxi, they switched bus drivers. At Mobile, the bus wobbled to a halt. The cabin lights came on, which caused people to groan and stir.

"We'll be here about forty-five minutes, folks. They have hot coffee and snacks inside." The bus driver tapped his cap and headed inside the terminal.

Shannon decided to go on a search for caffeine and protein.

Matt grunted. "Mind if I join you? I'm kinked up and need to walk."

"Not at all."

He slipped the straps to his laptop case onto his shoulder and motioned with his hand. "Ladies first."

She rolled her eyes but smirked. "Are you being a gentleman, or is it because I have the aisle seat?"

"Both. I could use a real meal. Not day-old donuts or a bag of chips. How about you?"

She agreed. They wandered into the predawn and stared at the metal building. Not much else lay around them. It seemed to be an industrial part of the city, and nothing seemed open this time of the early morning. Her stomach growled its disappointment.

"Well, there may be vending machines inside with peanuts or something." Matt shrugged.

Then she spotted the tell-tale marquee of a reputable fast food restaurant about a block down on the other side of the street. "There. They'll be open. A real, hot breakfast."

She glanced both ways down the street, which appeared to be void of traffic, then dashed across to the other curb. Matt's footsteps sounded behind her as he grabbed her elbow. "Wait up. This doesn't appear to be an area of town for a young lady to be waltzing around in by herself. Especially at this hour."

"True. Sorry." She slowed and placed her hand over her waist. "My stomach overruled my brain."

They walked in silence down the rutted path to the fast-food place. Obviously, many a traveler had traipsed this way to and from the bus terminal over the years. An open field lay off to their right behind a rusty fence. The winter grass tufts reached through the links and tickled her ankles.

The bright lights inside the restaurant jolted her senses. It took her a moment of squinting to read the overhead menu. She settled on a cup of coffee and a chorizo, egg, and cheese taco. Matt chose two bacon, egg, and cheese ones. He fisted his chest. "Can't eat sausage like I did when I was younger."

As they munched their breakfast and sipped their coffee, Matt again perused the internet. His finger swiped the mouse pad in circles, then he glanced at her. "I saw you slip that family money. Nice gesture."

She felt her cheeks warm. "Before I met you, I wouldn't never consider giving cash to a homeless person."

He bent to view his screen closer as he responded. "Understandable. Many people feel they will only waste it on drugs and alcohol, so it is like supporting their habit.

And many of them do just that."

"Then there are stories of people making lawyer-equivalent salaries by begging and never paying any taxes."

"Urban legends, mostly." Matt's eyes shifted to her then back to his computer. "Though rare, it does happen. Even so, besides the not paying the taxes part, which I don't condone, by the way, standing on street corners for twelve to fourteen hours a day in all sorts of weather is tough work. So is scrambling for a bed in a shelter. Only about a third waiting in line get inside. The rest are declined."

"Why?"

"No room at the inn."

His biblical reference didn't escape her.

He tapped the screen. "Found something else. It's not much, but it seems Manuel Andersen does have a track record of employment-seeking according to the state. There is no state income tax in Florida to track, but he did use their job-search database and put in his application for benefits with the employment commission."

"Can you tell where he worked? I mean, did some company hire him?"

"No. I don't have high enough clearance to determine that. But the fact that eighteen months ago he was searching for work in Tallahassee is a good sign."

She leaned back. "I am further in your debt. I'm going

to text Jayden."

Matt's shoulders lifted slightly as he took a sip of his coffee and downed the rest of his taco. "I'll forward this page to your email address if that's okay?"

How did he . . . oh, of course. Her business card. She nodded as she texted her husband.

Jayden pinged her back with a thumbs-up emoji. *Be there in four hours.*

She smiled as her thumbs clicked the response. *I'll be arriving about the same time. Meet me at the bus station? That way I won't have to get a cab.*

Then she giggled with her hand over her mouth as she read his response. *Only if I can embarrass you in public by sweeping you off your feet with a huge smooch.*

She recalled the famous photo of a sailor doing that to a woman at the end of WWII in New York City. Romantic, enduring. *Maybe, just this once . . .*

He sent her a wide-grinned happy face and two valentine emojis.

Her heart swelled as she clicked off, then she noticed Matt grinning at her.

"How long did you say you two have been married?"

"Six years, why?"

"You're still blushing like a bride. Nice to see in this day and age."

She swiped a curly strand of hair to hook behind her

ear and dropped her gaze to her lap. A small red and white envelope appeared on her phone with a number one beside it. "Thanks for the email."

"We'd better head back, or they may leave without us."

"Right." Shannon grabbed the leftover papers and cups and tossed them in the trash as they dashed out into the predawn morning. They were the last to board and ignored the arched brow of the bus driver as they mounted the steps.

Shannon snickered when they returned to their seats. "You're a bad influence on me, you know."

He gave her a "who, me?" gesture, re-opened his laptop, and changed his screen to a computer video game.

She laughed.

"Hey, my son got me hooked. We play it together. A way to stay in touch."

She wiggled her eyebrows. "Good to see in this day and age."

Matt's laughter echoed throughout the cabin, causing several groans and hushing sounds.

"Oops." His ears disappeared into his shoulders.

She glanced out the window and caught a highway marker. "Hey, they'll wake up in a few anyway. That sign read thirty miles to Pensacola."

Then her heart dropped. Her sweet and helpful friend

would be disembarking soon.

As if he read her mind, he extended his hand. "Nice meeting you, Shannon. I meant it, if you need anything else in your search, call me or email me. Okay? I'll be in the office today, and maybe a bit tomorrow."

"On Saturday?"

He huffed a breath. "Being at that convention for three days, I have a lot of paperwork to catch up on."

She bobbed her head. How many times had she spent Saturdays at her office going over the books, sending thank you emails to clients, or marketing on social media?

"Maybe you and your Jayden can swing by Pensacola on your way home. I'd like to meet this amazing man who captured your heart and to learn about your findings."

"Perhaps we can."

Satisfied, he returned to his game as Shannon swiveled to watch the world go by from the window across the aisle.

A little while later the bus turned into the terminal. Matt rose, gathered his things, and nodded goodbye. "Stay in touch. You will be in my prayers."

"Thank you again, Matt. For everything."

He locked gazes with her, then blinked and walked to the front of the bus.

She scooted to the window seat, still warmed by his body. Then she saw him stop at the curb and wave before heading inside.

Shannon gestured back and then settled her spine against the backrest. Only a few people boarded, fewer than had gotten off. No one sat beside her the rest of the way. She closed her eyes and dozed until they pulled into Tallahassee.

Chapter Ten

Jayden stood by the sidewalk, handsome as ever. The sight of him never grew old. And he was a man of his word. He swooped her into his arms, bent her backward, and planted a long kiss on her lips, which caused several cat whistles and handclaps.

When he finally released her, he walked her to his rig. "Tell me about this Matt fellow."

Shannon detected a touch of jealousy in his voice. Kinda sweet that he'd be a tad concerned. "He was a widower in his fifties, plays video games with his grown son in Atlanta, has a daughter in Belgium about our age, and another in Chicago, I think. And, since he works for the state of Florida as a social worker, he had oodles of connections. He found out several leads on Manny. He emailed them to me and said to drop his name if we hit any roadblocks."

Jayden stopped and raised both hands. "Whoa. Slow down. Take a breath, girl."

She did.

He pecked her cheek and opened the door to the passenger side of his cab.

Shannon climbed inside, knowing her cheeks revealed her pleasure in being with him.

He winked and closed the door. Then he went around to the driver's side, hoisted himself up into the seat, and turned the ignition.

She ran her hand over his muscular bicep. "I missed you."

His smile reached passed his cheeks. "Back at ya. Let's grab some lunch and then hit the motel. I bet we could both use a nice long shower."

She slipped her arm through his. "Hotel first, then eat?"

He clicked his tongue. "There you go, messin' with my mind again."

They both laughed as he pulled from the curb and geared up the rig.

Sitting cross-legged on the bed, surrounded by takeout

boxes of Chinese food, Shannon explained to Jayden about the halfway house and the employment commission.

"You think either of these places will speak to us? I mean, aren't there privacy laws and all?"

She dug a piece of sweet and sour chicken out with a pair of chopsticks and chewed before responding. "Matt said to contact him if we ran into any barriers. He'll be in the office today and some tomorrow."

"In Pensacola, right?"

"Right, but I think he has a good amount of clout. And he stated he often comes here to Tallahassee on business, probably because it is the state capital, so . . ." She pumped her eyebrows up and down.

Jayden sighed. "Well, guess we better finish lunch and head out. I don't want to take the rig, so I'll call for an area driver to pick us up."

Shannon slapped her head. "I didn't even think about that."

Her husband pecked her cheek. "It's okay, girl. I've got this. Found a coupon online. You go get dressed and I'll schedule one."

She smiled at this thoughtfulness. Jayden may have his quirks, and this job situation did snag her nerves, but he was the husband God chose for her. She knew it. She needed to show him that fact more often than she had been lately.

An hour later, they stood on the covered porch of the Better Life Ahead facility. The early twentieth-century, Craftsman-styled home had been converted into living quarters to house the resident men. The house next door had been as well, according to the sign. A second-story, covered catwalk, stretched over the driveway, connected the two.

Shannon glanced at Jayden as he rang the doorbell. The warmth of his hand clasping hers reassured her. She'd have hated to do this on her own. She realized more than ever how much she needed him, though all too often she convinced herself otherwise when he traveled for weeks on end earning a living so her dream of owning her own business could thrive.

Footsteps sounded inside, growing louder. The door opened to reveal a middle-aged man who could have easily played professional football in his youth. His eyes scanned them.

"Yes, can I help you?"

Jayden spoke first. "We hope you can. My wife and I have come from Texas to locate a long-lost relative of a church friend."

Shannon dug out Matt's business card and pressed it against the screen door. "Another friend of ours, Matt Kilpatrick, who is a state social worker, discovered on his internet search that this relative may have been a resident here several years ago."

The man scrutinized the card, and then them again. "I see. And you want to know what happened to him?"

"Yes, sir. If that is possible. Matt explained that you help them get back on their feet. He also discovered Manny had applied for assistance with the employment commission."

He stepped back. "Manny? Manuel Andersen?"

The tightness in Shannon's chest eased. "Yes. His aunt who raised him, Grace Perkins, is . . ." She couldn't bring herself to say the word dying, as if somehow that would usher in the inevitable quicker.

Jayden finished her sentence. "She is in hospice and probably doesn't have very long. She wants to see her nephew one last time."

Either her husband's words or the expression on her face must have melted any doubt in the man's mind. He opened the screen and ushered them inside. "Come in. My office is through the door on the right."

The house appeared as if an army of maids had just left. A slight whiff of pine cleaner and wood polish hung in the air. Shannon stopped and peered into the large room to the left. An area rug lay over the hardwood floors. Several chairs and couches gathered around a stone fireplace, flanked by two bookshelves. Above the shelves, the afternoon sun filtered through diamond-shaped window panes, obviously original to the structure. Framed posters with positive messages decorated the walls. "That's the parlor where we have our morning Bible study. The office is this way."

The office, probably once a dining room, opened via French doors.

"I'm Bob Martin." He shook their hands and motioned them to have a seat in the chairs that perched in front of a massive wooden desk. "Manny ended up being one of our best success stories. In fact, he stayed on until last year as my custodian. Then we both felt it was time for him to go back into the world and try to make it." He scooted his chair closer to a computer screen angled at the corner of the desk. "I got an email from him about six months ago, as I recall. But it didn't say much. I haven't heard from him since then."

Shannon glanced around the room. A bookcase housed various awards and plaques as well as a few books and knickknacks. A framed poster depicting Philippians 4:13, "I can do all things through Christ who gives me strength," painted on a brick wall in graffiti style, hung on the wall next to a window facing the street. A rendition of a man with a sledgehammer, falling into the arms of Jesus, hung behind the desk. She caught her husband's attention and motioned to it with her eyes.

His face eased into a smile. He mouthed the word

"nice."

"Ah, here we are." The man shifted his eyes from the screen back to them. "To make sure we are speaking about the same person, do you have his date of birth?"

"Yes, we do." She handed him the copy of his birth certificate. "We also spoke to his ex-wife, Martha Walters."

Mr. Martin arched an eyebrow. "I see."

"Her voice still held some residual anger, but she became quite open and helpful with what information she could provide." Shannon reached into her purse. "We also have this. An old friend of Mrs. Perkins in Fort Meyer sent it to her." She unfolded the news clipping and handed across the desk.

As he read it, she continued. "We now know he was exonerated of the crime. But it did take its toll, from what we gather."

He leaned across the desk to hand it back. "You realize he became a street person after that, right?"

"We figured as much." Jayden scooted forward in his chair. "We know he was admitted to the hospital here in Tallahassee for malnutrition and dehydration at one point about twenty years ago."

"Ah, you have been doing your research. Very well. I know Matt, and if he trusted you enough to give you this much information, I can be candid with you. However, without Manny's permission, I cannot discuss his treatments and stay here or provide any details about my correspondence with him since he left."

"We understand." Shannon retrieved the clipping and refolded it, putting it back in the plastic bag. As she did, a poof of Mrs. Perkins's lavender cologne released from the creases, as if to remind her of the urgency. "But any information you can give us that could lead to his current whereabouts would be greatly appreciated, Mr. Martin. His aunt doesn't have much time left on this earth, though when God calls her home is known by Him alone."

"Right. And please. Call me Bob." Bob leaned back, tenting his fingers to his chin. "It is the same Manny Andersen. He had started down a wrong road before the robbery, but that incident definitely gave his descent momentum. Led to his divorce, which he told me ended up being a very nasty one."

"His ex-wife said he drank a lot after he came back from the war in the Middle East."

"And continued to do so for many years until he was, shall we say, persuaded to discharge from the Navy. Floated from one menial job to the next." Bob's chair creaked as he swiveled it. "He was admitted here by his own free will after being released from the hospital that last time in 2014. The man had been on the streets for more than two decades off and on, and I don't have to tell you what that does to the mind and the body. Something in him snapped though and allowed the mercy of Christ to seep in the first few months of his residency here. During his stay, the pent-up anger he harbored over things that happened in his life slowly unbound from his heart. He left a very different person with good job prospects. We helped him find an efficiency apartment close to downtown where he would most likely find permanent employment as a custodian and gave him a glowing reference letter." He took a sticky note from a dispenser near the edge of the desk and wrote on it.

Jayden gave Shannon a thumbs up. She widened her eyes in hope.

Bob handed her the square, yellow paper. "Here is the last known address I have for him. Part of our program's stipulation is that they return on a weekly, and then monthly, basis to our support group and Bible study. But as I said, he went from being in treatment to being one of my employees for a while. When he finally left, I think he wanted a fresh start. After a few emails, he decided it best to end all contact. It happens."

"Does that worry you?" Shannon scooted forward in her chair.

He chuckled. "At times. But it is also a good sign. We are a crutch, but we don't want to become a permanent handicap for these men. They need to learn to walk the streets of life again on their own. I am confident that is what Manny has done." He rose and extended his hand. "Good luck. I will pray that you find him in time."

Shannon and Jayden also rose, shook his hand, and turned to leave. He escorted them to the front door and peered out through the screen. "I don't see your car."

"We don't have one. I came on the bus, and my husband," Shannon touched his arm, "drives a rig. He is taking a few days off, so he doesn't have a load, but we didn't think it would be wise to drive his employer's cab around town."

Jayden retrieved his cell phone. "We'll call the driving service again. It shouldn't take them long to come get us. If you don't mind us sitting on your stoop."

Bob thought for a moment. "That can get fairly pricey. I may have a better idea. Wait here." He disappeared back inside the house.

Part of her wanted to leave, but curiosity cemented her feet. "What idea could he possibly have?"

Jayden's shoulders lifted then lowered. His expression held the same question. He began to stroll down the steps. Shannon followed. They both stopped on the lowest one and leaned against the wrought iron banister.

Somewhere the sound of a lawnmower's engine sputtered to life and two men appeared by the driveway with hand clippers ready to tackle the Ligustrum bushes that flanked the side of the house. Another followed behind with a rake and black plastic bag. From out of nowhere, two more came with buckets and sponges. They began to scrub the window shutters and frames.

Jayden whistled. "These men truly earn their keep around here. We'd better stay out of their way." He led Shannon back to the porch and stopped near the front door.

They heard the clunk of Bob's loafers and then the hinges on the screen complain as it opened.

"Sorry for the noise. Afternoon Bible study in the other house is over and now the men finish their chores." He came onto the porch and handed them a set of car keys. "Make you a deal. You drive the four men waiting by the garage into town to sell their baked goods and you can have the van for the next three hours. Here is the address where you drop them off. It is five blocks from Manny's last known address. But you must have them back here by six sharp."

Jayden's mouth opened but no words came out.

Shannon sputtered her thanks.

Bob brushed it away. "I will need a copy of your driver's license and insurance, though."

"Not a problem." Jayden lifted his wallet from his back pocket, flipped through to locate both documents, and handed them to Bob. "And as a thank you, we will fill the tank on the way back this evening."

Bob grinned as he tapped the requested info onto his palm. "I knew I could trust you two. Be right back."

He went to make the photocopies and then returned a few minutes later. "Here you go. Can I have a cell phone number, too?"

They both gave him theirs. He wrote the information down and smiled. "Thanks. Hope your search proves to be fruitful. If you find him, tell him I said hi and to drop by sometime for a chat. I'd love to catch up with him." He leaned in and cupped his hand to the side of his mouth. "He's always been one of my favorites."

"How many men do you help out here?"

"We can take in sixteen at a time, eight in each house. I live across the street." He pointed to a modest one-story, bungalow-styled home.

The three shook hands. As Jayden and Shannon walked down the driveway, the men working on the bushes waved at them. Four others waited by the opened garage, two holding baskets of baked goods. They smiled a greeting and climbed inside the van.

Jayden assisted Shannon into the front passenger seat then rounded the hood to get in the driver's side. Buckled up, he shoved the key in the ignition. "Everyone ready?"

A chorus of male voices replied that they were. As they pulled out, Jayden introduced himself and Shannon. The men cheerfully replied, each revealing their first names. Carl, Fasid, Anton, and José.

Shannon's initial angst began to loosen even more. Would they find Manny this afternoon? *Could it really be this simple?*

Leaf Me Alone

Chapter Eleven

Shannon didn't have the heart to tell Jayden she'd already consumed a mini loaf of banana nut bread in the past twenty-four hours. The aroma of the freshly baked goods enveloping the interior of the van had been way too tempting for her man. But did he have to buy three? Well, maybe she could take one for the bus ride back and the rest he could take on the road with him.

As he chatted with the men about the recent ball game scores, the thought of them having to say goodbye tomorrow evening dampened her mood. Each time, it became more and more difficult to do it. She had hoped by now she'd have gotten used to his leaving. Not a chance. If they ever decided to have kids, how hard would it be on them? Perhaps that's why they avoided that topic. Sure, Jayden made great money, but at what cost? Her biological clock ticked a bit louder. But she didn't know how to broach that topic with him.

One of the men guided them to the spot downtown where they should be let off. They agreed to meet back there at six. As they pulled away from the curb and waved goodbye to the men, Jayden gave her a brief glance. "You've been quiet. What's on your brain, girl?"

"This is all falling together so easy."

He scoffed. "Too easy?"

"Is that wrong? I mean God can open doors and clear paths. And if there is anyone whom He would shine down His favor upon, it would be Mrs. P."

He patted her knee. "Now, hon. You know our Lord doesn't play favorites. But I know what you mean."

She flashed him a soft smile. "So, according to my phone app, we turn right at the next block."

"Ten-four, back door." He flicked on his blinker. A few minutes later they edged in front of a large house that had been converted into several residences. The painted wooden marquee in the front yard read Brentwood Place. A no vacancy sign hung below it. The front yard had been mostly converted to house six concrete parking spaces. Only one car occupied it. Jayden pulled into the slot closest to the porch.

"Well, here goes nothing." Jayden unclicked his safety belt and then came around to help Shannon from the van.

They strolled hand in hand up the front walk. Four

numbered mail slots hung to the left of the door. No names.

"How do we let someone know we are here?" Shannon didn't see an intercom system.

"I haven't a clue. Wait here." Jayden clunked down the steps and walked around the building.

Shannon perched on the stoop, her knees bent to her chin. What did he search for?

A few minutes later he returned and shook his head. "I don't see any signs of life. Maybe everyone is at work."

Okay, so not so easy after all. "Should we leave a note?"

"Couldn't hurt I guess." He joined her on the stoop as she fished a notepad from her purse. She spoke as she wrote.

We are looking for Manuel Andersen. We have news about his family he should know about. Please call 210-555-9481 today or tomorrow. Thanks. Jayden and Shannon Johnson.

Jayden nodded his approval. She folded the note and slipped it into the small wedge between the front door and the jamb.

"Now what?"

Jayden pushed back his sleeve. "It's twenty after three. We could check out the employment commission."

"Worth a try." She took his hand, and he lifted her onto her feet. They walked back to the van. "Maybe we should pray as we ride. I am guessing they won't be as forthcoming as Bob was."

Jayden winked at her. "We have neglected to do that, haven't we? You pray. I'll drive."

After he started the engine, she bowed her head and began to thank God out loud for leading them this far and asked for Him to guide their words and actions.

By the time she had finished her short pleas, they had driven to the block where the employment commission building sat. They walked into the stark, glass-windowed building and scoped it out. Various kiosks covered one side of the lobby where people of all shapes, sizes, and races searched for leads. To the other side, seven desks checkered the industrial-green carpeted area. A sign told them to take a number and be seated. Jayden snatched one from the dispenser and motioned for them to head for the row of plastic chairs lining the windows. All were taken except for one. He let Shannon have it and stood next to her.

A digital display showed the number 162.

Shannon glanced at the paper Jayden held. 170. She sat back with a sigh and lifted her cell phone from her bag.

The sound of someone clearing her throat caught her attention. A middle-aged woman with her hair pulled tightly into a bun pointed to another sign. No cell phones allowed.

She grimaced and slid it back into her purse.

Jayden ran his hand down his face. From the dancing in his eyes, she could tell he had a hard time not bursting out laughing. He leaned down to her ear. "Typical government agency."

She put her finger to her lips and made a hushing sound.

A soft ding echoed throughout the room—163.

A man in torn jeans hanging down to his hips and a crumpled T-shirt rose and sauntered over to a desk where a woman half-rose from her chair. Shannon hated to judge but as someone seeking employment, she thought he'd have dressed a bit better.

She caught the expression on Jayden's face and figured he thought the same.

Another ding—164. A lady bounced a fussy child on her knee as the tot proceeded to throw a snack bag of cereal on the floor. Shannon rose, retrieved the bag and handed it to the mother.

The woman grunted and snatched it from her with a glare.

Shannon backed away and returned to her seat. A few more numbers passed, then 167. The woman hoisted the squiggly kid on her hip, walked to the next desk and shot Shannon one more sneer.

Jayden's hand rubbed her shoulder. "Don't let it get to

you."

Finally, 170 appeared on the screen. The two rose and headed to the back of the room where a Hispanic man with graying temples stood.

He extended his hand. "Ignacio Hernandez. Are you both seeking employment, because if so, you should have each taken a number."

Jayden again spoke for them both. "No, sir. Actually, we have a rather odd request. We are looking for someone who may have used your services a few years ago. We are trying to locate him to let him know his aunt is dying and wants to see him before . . ." He stopped and swallowed.

The official narrowed his gaze.

Shannon removed Matt's card from her wallet. "Matt used his database to discover he applied for assistance here. He said if you have any questions, you can contact him at the state office in Pensacola."

Mr. Hernandez took the card from her, read it and handed it back. "Then he should know we cannot reveal who our customers are."

Her heart drooped.

Jayden coughed into his fist. "We'd hoped you might give us some information. I know you don't know us from Adam, but I assure you all we want to do is contact him, let him know of his aunt's request, and then return to her bedside in San Antonio."

"I wish I could assist you. There are some agencies you can solicit to do background checks in order to find out information for you, but you won't get it from us. Unemployment records are held in strict confidence."

Jayden let a long breath out from his nostrils and extended his hand. "Thank you all the same."

Shannon sputtered a "but", then closed her mouth at her husband's warning glare. She ducked her head and pocketed Matt's card.

The two walked slowly from the agency back out into the late afternoon sunlight. Jayden leaned against the van. "Well, girl?"

"I don't know. I honestly don't. I guess go back to the apartments and see if anyone pulls up."

As if on cue, her cell phone chimed. She punched the speaker button. "Hello?"

A female voice answered. "If you are looking for Manny Andersen, he moved out six months ago suddenly without any notice. Left a note that he got a job as a janitor at the Tallahassee Museum and found a place closer to it." Click.

Shannon stared at her husband.

"Okay, we head there."

Shannon noticed the time on her phone read 4:32 p.m. "Do we have time? We have to pick the men back up at six."

He keyed in the name on his phone. "It's about fifteen minutes from here. Worth a try."

"Okay. Thanks, hon."

He opened the van door for her.

As they navigated the traffic, her cell phone rang. She stared at the caller ID. "It's Mrs. Perkins."

Jayden glanced at her with a puzzled expression.

"Hello? Mrs. Perkins?"

"Shannon, dear. Bailey tells me you are in Florida searching for Manny."

"Yes, ma'am. We are. We have some good leads."

"We?"

Her voice sounded weak. Shannon tried to cover her concern with an upbeat tone. "Yes, my husband, Jayden is with me. He took a few days off to help out."

"Oh, my. Tell him, thank you. I wanted you to know I recalled something. It came to me in a dream last night. Manny always wanted to be a janitor growing up. I don't know why."

Shannon stifled a laugh. "He may be one now. We are heading to what could be his place of employment."

"Oh, that's wonderful. I'll say a prayer." Her voice took on a shakiness. "But Shannon, hurry back."

"What's going on, Mrs. P.?"

"I think someone snuck into my room again last night. They may have drugged me. But I can't be sure. When I woke up it was near lunchtime."

A jolt of fear zapped her heart. "Is anything missing?"

"Not that I can see, dear. But the lady next door passed in the night. That makes four in a week."

"Well, maybe you heard the nurse coming in to give you your medication in the IV."

She sighed. "I guess. But, Shannon., yesterday afternoon we had a great talk and laughed together over memories. We read the Bible together. Her cheeks had a rosy hue to them, and she even went for stroll in the garden. It doesn't make sense that six hours later she'd be gone."

A creepy sensation shot up Shannon's arms. "Well, I've heard sometimes people rally before . . ." She didn't know how to finish her sentence.

"Yes, that is exactly what the nurse said to me. Forgive me. I'm being a silly old woman. Take care, and again thank your husband for me."

Before she could respond, Mrs. Perkins disconnected the call. Shannon stared at the phone for a few seconds.

"Is everything all right, hon?" Jayden peered into her eyes then back at the cars creeping bumper to bumper in front of him as they crawled along Highway 373.

"I'm not sure. What's that saying? I feel as if someone has stepped over my grave?"

He clucked his tongue. "Maybe we should stop and get you some water."

"No. I'm fine."

But deep inside her gut, she felt anything but that.

Chapter Twelve

"No, you're not fine, girl. Your face looks all squished to the center, which means you're thinking deep thoughts."

Shannon craned to view her reflection in the rearview mirror. Oh, yeah. Her face did resemble a raisin. She purposely relaxed her cheeks and forehead muscles. "They lost another one."

Jayden shot her a glance then returned his eyes to the highway. "Who lost what?"

"The hospice facility. Another resident passed in the night."

He wagged his head. "So?"

"Mrs. P. thinks someone tiptoed into her room in the wee hours of the morning and drugged her."

"Hon, it is a hospital, kinda, right? I mean nurses would check on their patients and she is on pain meds."

Shannon moved her neck side to side to relieve the

tension. "True, but I wonder . . ."

"What?" His question contained a tad bit of frustration.

Yes, she probably saw shadows where there were none but even so, an eerie sensation trickled down her spine. "I wonder if losing four patients in a week is, well, normal."

"For an end-of-life-facility?" He scoffed. "Um, yeah."

"You're right. Never mind." But she did mind. Something didn't seem right. She couldn't justify the inkling that tapped on her brain. Could it be a premonition, woman's intuition, or something from a higher source?

Once Shannon had been an impulsive person. If it popped into her head, she acted immediately. But in the past few years, partially thanks to Mrs. P.'s lessons, she had learned to step back and wait. Ask for confirmation or seek a sign to proceed. Each time she had, she found it had been a wise decision. Didn't a proverb talk about fools rushing in? Even so, something in her mentor's voice concerned her. Maybe she could phone Bailey later when Jayden was in the shower and get her opinion.

"There it is."

Jayden's voice jerked her back to the here and now. As he exited, she peered through the windshield to a small building tucked in a forest of tall, straight trees. A few cars dotted the small parking lot. It had a quaint and friendly appearance. Almost like an Old-West store in the movies, except made of modern materials.

They parked and walked to the covered porch. Glass doors, displaying the hours and a few other announcements of special events, greeted them.

"Well. Let's go see what we can find out." Jayden winked and pushed the door open for her.

They entered and walked to the information booth. A young woman gave them a warm smile.

"Welcome to the Tallahassee Museum. Is this your first visit?"

"Um, yes." Jayden glanced at the brochures then back at the docent. "But we're not here to tour, though it looks fascinating." His eyes scanned the room of glass-encased exhibits and more rustic, pioneer-themed displays.

Shannon decided to bail him out. "We are here to speak to one of your employees concerning his aunt who is not long for this world. She sort of commissioned us to find him and give him her final wishes."

The woman's hand went to her throat and fumbled the beads on her choker necklace. "I, uh . . . who is it you are wanting to speak with?"

"His name is Manuel Andersen. We understand he is on your custodial staff."

Her gaze darted as if not wanting to make eye contact. "Let me see if the facilities manager is available. He can probably assist you better than I could." She gave them a quick grin and excused herself from behind the booth.

Jayden rolled his eyes and, with his hands clutched behind his back, strolled over to an exhibit about how ants create their nests. When did he become interested in that?

Shannon let out a large sigh and joined him.

A woman with a group of school kids, all dressed alike, entered. Their excited, trill voices echoed off the shiplap walls. She hushed them with the teacher stare and her finger pressed to her lips. Then she told them to all hold hands and not to touch a thing or else. From their faces and immediate reaction, Shannon gathered they understood what the "or else" would be.

Shannon made eye contact with the teacher. "The docent went to locate the facilities manager for us. I'm sure she will be back shortly."

"Ah, well. That's fine." Her expression conveyed that it really was not at all. "Children, let's go see the red dinosaurs on the lawn."

Squeals and jumping in excitement pursued, along with high-pitched chattering. She ushered them back through the glass doors.

"Must be Tiger Cubs. I think they admit girls now." Jayden nodded as they left.

"You were in scouting, right?"

"Yep. Until I graduated from high school. Got razzed about it a lot, but then I got my Eagle and had letters of congratulations from the governor *and* the president of the United States. When the state attorney general showed up at my ceremony to present me a flag that had been flown over the state capitol in my honor, I got a bit more respect." He stuck his hands deep into his pockets. "It gave me street cred."

"Where is all that stuff now? Not in our apartment, I know."

"No, Mom has it boxed up, I guess."

She punched him in the arm. "Jayden Johnson. When we go see them for Thanksgiving, we are leaving with that box. I want that flag displayed in our home and those letters preserved in a memory album on our coffee table."

He shuffled his feet. "Okay."

The soft steps of the docent ended their conversation. She came up to them. "Mike is busy over in the alligator pond area. But he says Manny doesn't come on duty until after we close, which"—she glanced at her watch— "is in ten minutes."

Shannon figured that was a hint for them to leave. But they were not the only customers at the museum. "There seems to be a scout troop here for a tour."

The docent blanched. "Oh, my. They were scheduled to be here at three-thirty."

Jayden motioned with his thumb. "They headed over to see the red dinosaur sculpture."

She asked them to excuse her and dashed out the door.

Shannon turned to her husband. "So, do we wait in the car?"

"I guess. Or go find the alligators."

She held up her hands in surrender. "Ah, you can go do that. I'll go wait in the van."

He chuckled and clicked the fob to open the doors, then opened the door for her. He closed the door and then motioned he planned to walk the grounds in search of the facilities manager.

Shannon settled into the passenger seat, cracked the window, and gazed at the tall trees, some with moss dangling from their branches. Didn't have any like these in San Antonio. Texas trees sprawled with twisted branches. Now she understood where those smelly, tar-coated phone poles came from. Though she gathered that with more and more optic underground cables, they were going the way of the red dinosaur that had all the scouts so mesmerized.

Ten minutes later, she noticed Jayden wandering toward her at an easy pace. He waved and got in the van.

"Well?"

"He works here. Has for six months, just as our anonymous caller stated. Reports to work at six. That's when we are picking up the men. I gave the manager our names and your cell phone number. He said he would give it to Manny."

Shannon's hopes sank. "There isn't any more we can do, then. Let's pray he calls us."

Jayden started the engine. "Right."

"So, what do we do for an hour?"

He chuckled. "If this was my rig, I'd tell you. But it isn't our car, so . . ."

She felt her face heat. "Stop. You were better-behaved on our honeymoon."

He pouted, but in jest.

"I don't want to put miles on something that has been graciously loaned to us. I guess we head to the rendezvous spot and wait."

"Sure. We can get out and stroll around downtown. When the men see the van, they'll wait for us." He gave her a thumbs-up and pulled out onto the highway.

Shannon kept glancing in her side-view mirror. Two cars back, a black pick-up patterned their route. It had ever since they turned out of the museum. She'd noticed it coming down one of the side roads near the dinosaur sculptures.

Were they being tailed? Why?

"Jayden, I'm thirsty. Can you turn into that drive-through on the left?"

He glanced at the digital clock on the dash. "Okay. We've got a bit of time." Turning on his blinker, he eased over to the center, turn-only lane.

The truck veered to the left as well, but then it passed them. Shannon craned around her husband's shoulders to peer inside of it as it zipped by, but the windows were tinted. She detected only the shadow of a driver, no passenger.

Maybe her imagination. Probably lived in the neighborhood behind the restaurant. If a worker at the museum drove the mystery truck, it would make sense to live nearby.

But as Jayden headed into the drive-through, she noticed the pick-up turn onto a side street.

"Hon, um, pull into the parking lot. I need to use the ladies' room. Can I bring you something on the way back?"

"A hot coffee would be nice."

She opened the passenger door and slid out. "Okay. Back in a few."

When Shannon remerged, drinks in hand, her heart had stopped rat-tat-tatting in her chest, and she'd convinced herself she'd been over-dramatic. Jayden leaned across the seats to open the door for her. She passed the drinks to him to put in the cup holders, then climbed into the van.

As he backed out, she took a sip of her diet cola through the straw. It hit her tonsils and spewed back out.

There, in the parking lot behind the drive-through, sat the black pick-up . . . waiting.

Chapter Thirteen

"You okay?" Jayden slammed the brakes before exiting the fast food place. His wife acted as antsy as she did on their wedding day. Maybe a bit more. Not like her. She usually kept it all together in a tight package. She liked her world orderly.

"No, Jayden. We're being followed." She motioned with her head. "Black truck with the white racing stripe parked over by the drive-through speaker."

"What?" He lifted his chin to gaze into the rearview mirror. "You sure?"

A horn blasted. A red sports car behind them wanted to leave as well.

Jayden swallowed down the urge to get out and punch the guy. Instead, he waved and pulled back onto the road. The man in the sports car glared at him and shook his head as he revved his engine and zoomed past them on the right.

Jayden's jaw moved but he held his tongue.

Shannon didn't comment. Instead, she gazed into her side-view mirror. Bless her for knowing when to remain quiet. He felt his blood pressure inching back to normal. Until he noticed a flash of black in his rearview mirror.

"It's pulling out of the parking lot now. When did you first see it?"

"It left the museum when we did and has been holding back a few cars ever since." She dug into her purse for a tissue and brushed the soda fizz off her blouse.

"And you're just telling me this now?" His voice raised in pitch and volume as his angst hugged his throat. This day kept getting weirder.

"I wasn't certain."

He blasted a deep sigh through his nostrils the way his father used to when he didn't want to verbalize his thoughts. He always hated that gesture and yet, here he was doing the same thing.

She didn't respond. But her hands wrapped the tissue back and forth as she tucked her sweet lower lip in her teeth. So, she did need him after all. Of course, because right now Bailey and Jessica weren't around to confide in . . . no, man. Don't go there.

After a few moments of excruciating silence, he turned slightly toward her as he drove.

"Here's the plan. We keep heading for downtown.

Mind our own business and wait for the men." He angled his head toward the rear of the van. "If the driver of that truck stops when we do, I plan to confront him face to face and find out what he's up to." He pointed a finger at her. "And don't talk me out of it. I'll be careful. Promise."

"Is that wise? I mean, to confront him."

Jayden flared his nostrils and gripped the wheel tighter. *Ease it back down. She's just jumpy.*

Shannon wiped her mouth and wadded up the tissue, then turned to stare out of her window.

The temperature inside the van became considerably colder.

As soon as it rolled off her tongue, Shannon regretted it. The one thing a wife should never ask her husband is if his plan is wise. It is like sucker-punching his ego's solar plexus. Jayden stood six-one and easily weighed 190 pounds. All lean and muscle, though. Being on the road so much, he worked out at a gym every chance he could. Any stranger could tell her man had street cred for sure.

She bowed her head. "Sorry. Do what you think is best."

His thank you came out a bit terse.

So much for the romantic tête-à-tête. Marriage could be such an emotional tangle at times, and his being gone so much pulled on the threads that bound them. Not that she would ever entertain the idea their relationship would unravel, but it had some snags. She rubbed her eyebrow and returned her focus to the windshield.

"Whoever it is in the truck, he's still following us." His response spat out like bile.

Shannon bit down on her tongue. The tension in the van increased as the silence lingered all the way into the downtown area. Except for the thumping in her inner ears.

Downtown Tallahassee resembled many other cities, yet the lush trees and grassy areas lent to a serene sensation and greatly minimized the hustle and bustle of the large, populated capital. Not that many skyscrapers, either. They filled up the van's gas tank at a corner store then parked and wandered into a town square with a bubbling fountain. The truck continued past them and turned right.

"Good. He's gone. Let's sit over there, girl."

He led her by placing his hand on the small of her back. They decided on one of the benches near the fountain. The metal held the late afternoon sun's warmth like a child clinging to his mother on the first day of daycare. It felt good on the back of her legs.

"Hungry?"

He didn't wait for her response but wandered toward

a street-vendor cart. Jayden brought back a bag of popcorn, and they settled in to people watch. Perhaps he'd forgotten about the loaves of banana nut bread in the van. Though, how could he? The aroma penetrated it.

Oh, of course. The van. "Maybe it was the logo on the van made the guy curious?"

He jiggled a few popped kernels in his hand. "Yeah. You could be right. I hadn't thought about that."

Jayden's moodiness disturbed her. What did he not want to tell her? "Did something happen in Orlando?"

"Nothing you need to worry about." As if to signal the conversation was over, he shoved the snack into his mouth and turned his head.

Okay. She'd let it drop for now, but before he left tomorrow, she'd find out what was swimming around in his brain. She watched his eyes travel around the square as if he sized up every pedestrian. A woman held hands with her two small children as they hopped and skipped toward an ice cream truck, almost tugging her arms out of her shoulder blades. An older man, perched on a bench down the way, read a newspaper. Two businessmen strutted quickly as they chatted, and then jogged across the street to an office building.

No black truck.

After several minutes of silence, he turned to her. "Are you still worried about those people dying at the hospice place?" He handed her the bag after taking another handful himself.

"Sort of. I mean, I'd feel better if I knew the occurrences so close to each other were normal." She reached inside for some of the popcorn and plopped a few kernels in her mouth. The buttery saltiness did taste good.

"Hmm." He dug out his phone and spoke a command. "What is the average length stay in hospice?"

A pleasant female voice answered his question. "According to the website . . . the average stay is 19.2 days nationwide."

"There. Between two and three weeks."

Deep inside, it felt as if a large, meaty hand grabbed Shannon's chest and squeezed it. "Mrs. Perkins has been there five days. That means . . ." She swallowed through the sudden dryness in her mouth.

He rubbed her forearm. "Av-er-age. I'm sure many of them stay longer, girl. Some may just give up on life a day or so after they get there. Mrs. Perkins is a tough old lady. And didn't you tell me her doctors gave her a month? She could have longer."

She blinked back the shimmering in her eyes, which made the fountain in front of them look like an impressionistic period painting. "Yes, I know. I'm being silly. It could very well be those other folks checked in weeks before her."

"You're not being silly." His tone held a reprimand. "But yes, probably. What's the name of the facility again?"

"Golden Days."

He keyed it in. Their website popped up on the screen with a 4.8-star rating. He pointed to it. "There. It's a good place."

She gave him an attempt at a smile, which she knew fell short of convincing him that his brief research reassured her. "Let's talk about something else. Tell me more about getting your Eagle badge, isn't that what you called it? Sounds like a very big deal." She handed him the popcorn bag again, indicating she'd had her fill.

Pride washed over his features. He began to rattle about it. She half-listened, delighted in his accomplishment and wondering why in six years of marriage, or even the year they dated before that, he'd never mentioned it. Perhaps he had, and she hadn't listened . . . like now. She needed to try to pay more attention to her wonderful guy. Maybe things would be better between them if she did.

But the other half of her thoughts still spun with doubt. Not about her marriage, but about Mrs. Perkins' situation.

Was Golden Days as stellar as its ratings stated? Should she be concerned? She'd read somewhere —or maybe Jessica, who wrote for a living, told her—website comments were often skewed because companies hired less than scrupulous people to write made-up testimonies of praise.

Did her old, anxiety-driven what-ifs begin to surface despite her best efforts to squelch them? If so, she should simply ignore them, right? After all, the black truck incident had been much ado about nothing.

Or had it?

Something caught the corner of her eye. The black pick-up with the white stripe drove by them at a slower-than-normal-traffic rate.

Jayden's furrowed eyebrows told her he'd seen it as well. The almost empty bag of popcorn crunched into a ball in his hands. "That's it. I need to find out what this dude's problem is." He stood, two-point shot the wadded bag of popcorn into the receptacle like a basketball pro, and begin to strut toward the street.

Shannon reached out to him. "Wait. Here come the men." She sent up a fast prayer, thanking God for His timing.

Jayden shifted his attention across the street as the four men with mostly empty baskets waited to cross it.

"Right." He wiggled his open-palmed fingers to take her hand, still concentrating on the vehicle that kept surveying them. The black truck's engine revved as it increased its speed down the street.

Shannon slipped her hand into his and felt his gentle strength pull her to her feet. He wrapped an arm around her shoulder. "Let's go, girl. If that truck follows us all the way back to Better Life Ahead, he is going to have to explain things to more than just me."

When they reached the sidewalk of the square, Jayden clicked the fob to open the van's doors. He plastered on a grin and waved his hand over his head in the direction of their passengers.

They each acknowledged his greeting and shuffled to the vehicle, settling in the back seats with soft chatter.

Jayden helped Shannon into the van and then rounded the front to climb back into the driver's seat. As he clicked his belt, he twisted to the back. "How'd it go?"

"Sold all but two loaves." One of the guys, Carl, grinned and held up his basket.

"We sold all but one." Two others, Fasid and José held theirs up as well. "We had a good day."

"What do you do with the leftovers?" Jayden started the engine.

"Bob takes them to the Lighthouse Orphanage twice a week."

Shannon and Jayden exchanged smiles. Of course, he would.

As they pulled out of the downtown area, Jayden addressed the men again. "Say, can I ask you guys something? We noticed we got a few weird looks driving around in the van today."

Carl clucked his tongue. "Yeah, that happens. We get used to it. Some people recoil when we tell them who we represent. Man, they just don't get it. People make mistakes."

Fasid nodded. "They don't understand that we are trying to straighten out our lives."

"Yeah, they look at us like we are going to take the money to buy booze or something." His partner shook his head. "Or bonk them with our basket, snatch their money, and run."

The others chuckled. Anton spoke over the laughs. "We get used to the gawk, ya know, man?"

"Right." Jayden sighed. "Shame you have to, though. Turn here?" He pointed to the traffic light ahead.

"Yeah, man, then go four blocks," Anton responded with a head bob as his dreadlocks bounced off his shoulders. "At the four-way stop, take a right."

"Thanks. Did any of you know Manny Andersen?"

José sat back and folded his arms over his chest. "I did. Why?"

"We're looking for him. The aunt who helped raise him is dying and wants to see him one last time."

"Wow, that's tough." Anton clucked his tongue. "Tell him what he needs to know, José."

José's features softened. "Didn't know he had kin. Knew his wife left him and took the kid a long time ago."

Shannon spoke for the first time. "Yes, she spoke to us. Briefly. She told us his name is Parker."

"That's right." José scoffed. "Hey, my woman left me too due to the booze. Found a new man, just as his did, and split. We sorta related to our situations, ya know?"

Seems Martha Walters had a history as well, though she didn't reveal that information to Shannon, did she? Marriage break-ups are often two-sided. She swiveled her torso to better view the men. "We heard he's employed now at the museum. We went there, but he had not reported to work yet. Are you still in touch?"

"Nah. Not really. Though, I'd heard he got a good job and even bought a truck."

Jayden shot her a wide-eyed expression then lifted his chin to view José in the rearview mirror. "What kind?"

José protruded his lower lip. "Don't know, man. But if you wanted to bet me, I'd say black. It's his favorite color. He used to carry a picture of one with a white racing stripe in his wallet as inspiration."

The popcorn suddenly came together as one solid mass in Shannon's stomach and threatened to jolt into her mouth

Leaf Me Alone

.

Chapter Fourteen

After work, Bailey tiptoed down the hallway to Mrs. Perkins's room. Somehow being quiet around people in their last days seemed appropriate. She tapped on the partially opened door.

"Come in?" When Mrs. Perkins recognized her through the medicinal haze, a smile oozed across her wrinkled face. She motioned with the hand that didn't have an IV pump attached to it. "Ah, Bailey. How sweet of you to drop by."

Bailey eased closer to her and took her fingers. "Hi. I thought I'd come for a short visit if you are up to it."

The old woman scooted up further on her pillows with a strained effort. "Of course. I've just been doing a bit of reading."

A page-worn Bible sat open on her lap. *Wow, she still does that?* Bailey half expected her to have most of it memorized by now after all these years of teaching it. "What's your favorite?"

"Philippians, chapter 4 of course. The most read portion of the Good Book according to the statistics."

Bailey filed a reminder in her short-term memory to mark it on her phone app. Then one of the verses came to mind. "Oh, yeah. I can do all things through Christ who gives me strength, right?"

"Verse 13. Very good. But lately, I have been clinging to verses six and seven. 'Do not be anxious about anything, but in every situation, by prayer and petition, with thanksgiving, present your requests to God. And the peace of God, which transcends all understanding, will guard your hearts and your minds in Christ Jesus.'"

Bailey's heart tugged her breath. "Are you feeling anxious?"

Mrs. Perkins' bony shoulders raised a tad. "It's hard hearing about others passing on. Makes it all seem so real. I always thought I'd be ready when He called, but . . ."

She didn't know what to say, or how to say it. How do you give comfort to a woman who is so used to providing it for everyone else? "I, um, can't imagine."

"Of course, you can't." Wisdom shimmered in the tired eyes. "You're young." She reached over and tapped Bailey's hand. "And in love, yes?"

Her cheeks heated. Bailey rubbed one. "Maybe. I'm

not sure."

"Yes, you are. But it scares you. Love can be an overwhelming emotion. And I imagine the fact you lost your fiancé in Afghanistan makes you wary. Do you believe you are betraying his memory by letting another man into your heart?"

Bailey shifted her weight to her other foot. Here she'd come to comfort Mrs. Perkins, but the sweet lady instead ministered to her. "I'm not sure. But Chase and I have talked about that a bit."

The woman nodded. "Then he's a good man. Don't let another woman discover it, now."

That brought a laugh. More as a comic relief. Bailey cleared her throat. "Can I pray with you?"

A soft glow spread over the elderly cheeks. She closed her eyes and squeezed Bailey's hand. "I would like that very much."

The tongue in Bailey's mouth didn't want to cooperate. Why did she feel so nervous? She swallowed and silently asked the Holy Spirit to speak through her. But halfway through her prayer, the noise level in the facility increased.

Feet shuffled.

A voice wailed. "Help. Someone, help. She's not breathing."

A tear trickled down Mrs. Perkins' cheek. "That

sounds like Mary Beth. Poor dear. I guess her mom has gone on to be with Jesus. Sweet woman. Battled breast cancer off and on for over twenty years. Still, Mary Beth held onto the hope the doctors were wrong and her mother would beat it again."

The reality of life and death slammed hard against Bailey's chest. She didn't know what else to do but bow her head to hide the tears swimming in her eyes as well. Maybe she should do as Shannon's text suggested. Talk to Chase about the frequency of deaths in this place. But on the other hand, wasn't that why they all were admitted here?

She slipped through the halls as a heavy silence fell over the place. On the counter of the reception desk, a battery-operated candle sat inside a white, mesh wreath intertwined with a garland of silver stars. It had been lit to let others know someone had just passed. The fake flicker somehow soothed her as she eased out the glass doors into the real world where normal activity bustled without much thought of mortality issues.

The black truck appeared behind them again, but it eased into the commuter traffic. If it was Manuel Andersen driving, he likely recognized the way back to the shelter. Jayden let out a sigh. Surely, he'd make himself known later.

Wouldn't Jayden do the same? If a strange couple driving a van from a place he used to live during a not-so-great-time in his life started asking about him, he might wonder about their motives, too.

His wife kept quiet, but her sideways glances and scrunched eyebrows told him she wondered what rattled in his brain.

"It's not there now." He gave her a small wink. "If it does reappear, I'll act cool."

"Promise?"

"Yeah. Can't blame the dude for being curious. Besides, he probably headed on to work."

She leaned the back of her short afro against the headrest. "Guess if ghosts from my past edged into my here and now, I'd be a bit hesitant to find out why. Kinda like . . . what did my grandmother use to say? Waiting for the other shoe to drop?"

"Exactly what I was thinking." Jayden chuckled. "Always wondered what that saying meant."

"Comes from the ghettos of New York, man." Anton raised his voice to be heard over the van's engine. "The brownstones were not well insulated. When your neighbor upstairs kicked his shoe off, you heard the thunk and waited for the second one."

"Ah, because there had to be two. I get it, man." José bopped in his seat.

That started a conversation about noisy people, in prison and then at the halfway house. The four were laughing over someone named Artie whose snores could wake the dead. It ended in laugher as Jayden pulled into the driveway, shaking his head at their camaraderie and antics.

Bob Martin stood on the porch, waving. "How'd ya do?"

"All but three, boss," José yelled back with a huge, gold-toothed grin.

As the men clamored up the steps, Bob patted them each on the back. "Supper's on the table. It's spaghetti night."

He turned to Jayden who handed him the keys to the van. "You two are more than welcome to stay."

Jayden turned to Shannon. His silent "your choice" gesture caught her attention. Her eyes enlarged as if to ask why did it have to be up to her?

True. He was supposed to be the head of the household, after all. He broke their telepathy and returned his attention to Bob. "That's kind of you, but as a long-hauler, our time together is precious and limited." He slipped his arm over his wife's shoulders, suddenly feeling all gooey inside at the thought of her being his woman. God had blessed him.

A twinge of red seeped into Bob's cheeks. "Oh, yeah. Okay." He glanced at his feet for a second then back to them. "Did you have any luck locating Manny?"

Jayden smiled, touched by the man's awkward need to change the subject instead of coming back with some lewd remark like many of the truckers would. Decent dude. "Not really, but we got a good lead. Seems he is working at . . ."

"The Tallahassee Museum." Bob snapped his fingers. "I forgot he gave me as a reference, and they called on him about six months back. Sorry."

"It's cool." But inside Jayden became a tiny bit irritated that Bob hadn't recalled it sooner. Oh well, the man had a lot of responsibilities keeping sixteen ex-cons and former street people in line.

Shannon extended her hand. "We greatly appreciate all your help. He may have seen the van and be curious as to why it showed up at his place of employment, so if he contacts you, can you tell him why we're here? We are staying at the Starlight Motel."

Bob jutted his chin in recognition as he took it then repeated the gesture to her husband. "The one out on Highway 90?"

"Yeah, that's the one." Jayden gave Bob's hand a hearty shake.

"How are you planning to get there?"

Jayden showed him the private taxi service app on his phone.

Bob winked. "I have a better idea. Can you wait a minute?" He disappeared into his office before they could answer. A moment later he returned with a set of keys dangling from a chartreuse rabbit's foot. "Here. We had an old Honda donated to us a few months ago. It's not fancy, but it is in fairly good shape. Use it while you're here."

His unexpected kindness splashed against Jayden's chest like a sudden burst of ocean waves over a jetty. "Um, wow. I don't know what to say. You sure?"

Bob pressed a hand on his shoulder, though it meant him raising it since he stood several inches shorter than Jayden. "I have your driver's license and insurance info. You two seem like a nice couple on a good mission." He lowered his hand and shoved it into his jean's side pocket. "And, as I said earlier, Manny has a special place in my heart. Despite his age, he turned his life around. One of my major success stories, and we all need one of those, right? It keeps me going."

Shannon gave him a brief hug. "Thank you."

Jayden swallowed down the mild irritation that his wife drew close to another man. And the fact that her innocent gesture jerked his chain made him uncomfortable. He trusted her. Still . . . maybe it was natural for a little jealousy to live in the corner of a man's heart. Especially when he couldn't be a part of her day-to-day life. That revelation made him take a step back and take another look at what he did. Did the increase in income make it worth it? Maybe not. The uncertainty kept surfacing lately. Something he needed to pray about some more.

"We better go. Your dinner's getting cold." He motioned with his head toward the sound of chatter coming from down the hall.

Bob laughed. "I doubt it. I'll be lucky if they left me any. Which is why I always have frozen dinners across the street in the fridge." He opened the front door. "Car's parked in the back. Any other way I can help, let me know. And if Manny contacts me, I'll pass on your message."

Jayden pressed his hand to Shannon's back, indicating they should take their leave. She gazed up at him with one of her killer smiles, the kind that always melted him like butter on a fresh-out-of-the-oven slice of bread.

A few minutes later, they climbed into the Honda, which, speaking of bread, smelled faintly of banana nut.

Shannon slapped her forehead. "We left the loaves you bought in the van."

Jayden shrugged as he backed out of the driveway. "They'll find them on the console tomorrow. The orphans' gain."

"It's fine. My hips don't need it anyway."

His eyes scanned her slenderness. "Right,

supermodel."

Her long lashes lowered over her eyes as her hand playfully pushed his shoulder. "Stop." But her smile told him she hung onto his compliment like a precious memento.

Halfway to the motel, Shannon's phone chimed.

"Bailey." She held it out as if asking permission to answer it.

"Okay." He swallowed down the agitation. Maybe it irked him that his wife had such a close relationship with Jessica and Bailey. On the other hand, he really liked them and was grateful they kept her company while he traveled the roads. Women needed women. That's what Shannon had said. Probably true. Trouble being, men need women, too. And right now, knowing that black frilly thing sat in her suitcase pulled on his heartstrings.

He could hear the hum of Bailey's voice but not her words.

Shannon's voice shrilled. "What? Oh my. While you were there?"

Jayden knitted his brows and mouthed, "What?"

She pulled the phone from her ear. "Another woman passed at the hospice center while Bailey visited Mrs. Perkins." She punched a button on the front. "Bailey, I've put you on speaker. I'm riding with Jayden."

"In his rig?"

"No, we sort of borrowed a car. I'll explain later. So, go on. Tell us what happened."

"I'm not sure. I guess her daughter came to visit and found her, well . . . gone."

"Oh, Bailey, How awful."

Jayden glanced at the pained expression on his wife's face. He took her hand and squeezed it. "Was it expected?"

"I guess, Jayden. I mean . . ."

"Yeah. It's normal in a place like that. That's what I keep telling Shannon."

"So y'all don't think I should talk to Chase again about the number of people dying here?" Bailey's tone sounded worried and confused.

Shannon bit the side of her lip as she searched his face for the right answer. So, she did need him after all. He felt a manly surge run through his veins. Jayden gave his wife a thumbs up. "I trust your instincts. If you two think something weird is going on, then investigate it."

Shannon rubbed her eyebrow. "I don't know. It's probably nothing, Bailey. Maybe it is hitting us that soon it will be Mrs. P., and we are blowing it all out of proportion."

Bailey's sigh blasted through the speaker. Then her voice quivered. "Yeah. I guess. That's what Chase said, too. Any luck locating Manny?"

"A bit. Yes. We found out where he works and have left a message."

"Wow." Her voice elevated in pitch. "That's great. Good job, y'all. I'm calling Mrs. P.'s room now. That will cheer her up."

"Is she okay?" Shannon tucked her lip in her teeth again. Jayden patted her knee. He really wanted to pull over, hang up the phone, and take her in his arms . . . for a long time.

"Yeah, I guess. I mean, they are keeping her comfortable. Her speech seems a bit slurred, probably from the pain meds. I'll text you tomorrow. Have a good evening." Her voice sang-sung as if she sensed Jayden's desire to be alone with his wife. Did she? Did that mean Shannon wanted the same thing, and so the telepathy between friends extended all the way into Texas?

"Take care, Bailey." He leaned closer to the phone in his wife's hand. "Thanks for keeping us posted. We'll do the same."

"Tell Chase we said hi." Shannon smiled at the receiver.

"You two behave yourselves, now." Bailey chuckled and disconnected the call.

Jayden wiggled his eyebrows. "Food or . . ."

Shannon rubbed her stomach. "I'm still full of popcorn."

He grinned. Yeah, his thoughts exactly. Mrs. Perkins, Manny Andersen, and the rest of the world could wait until tomorrow. About time he spent some long, sweet, quiet hours alone with his wife.

Leaf Me Alone

Chapter Fifteen

That didn't happen. About nine o'clock, as Jayden and Shannon sat cross-legged on the bed devouring a sub sandwich, a knock pounded on their door.

Shannon jolted and drew her robe closer.

Jayden climbed off the bed and motioned with his hand for her to dash into the bathroom area.

She did, glanced around, and grabbed the iron from the shelf of the closet. Not much of a weapon, but if she swung hard enough it might knock someone out.

"Who is it?"

"Manuel Andersen. I believe you two are looking for me?"

She heard the hinges complain as Jayden opened the door. What was he doing? She peeked around the corner.

An older man with whitening hair stood on the stoop.

She heard her husband respond. "Yes. We are. Can

you wait a minute, though? My wife needs to get more presentable."

She snatched her jeans and blouse from the hanger and dashed into the small space housing the toilet and tub. She heard the front door lightly close and her husband's footsteps move toward her. A hanger tinkled. She gathered he grabbed his shirt. Then a tap came on the bathroom door.

"Hon?"

"I heard. I'll be right out."

She ran a hand down her clothes, puffed her curly hair, and slipped back into the room.

Jayden stood by the door, waiting for her nod.

"Okay."

He opened the door and motioned for the gentleman to enter. "Take a seat." He waved his hand toward the small round table with two chairs then edged over to Shannon, encasing her in his arm. She felt his warm strength and leaned into it, thankful he decided to help her on this search.

The older man glanced at them, but remained standing, his legs stiff and still. "You have a message from Aunt Grace?"

Shannon opened her mouth, but then closed it again when Jayden gave her arm a small squeeze as if to tell her he'd handle this. He dropped his hand to his side then walked over and extended it to their guest.

"Yes. I'm Jayden Johnson and this is my wife Shannon. We belong to her church and she teaches the Bible to my wife and her friends."

Manny crossed his arms in a pretzel over his chest instead of shaking Jayden's hand. "So?"

Jayden lowered his arm. Shannon saw his jaw twitch, but his voice remained even. He backed up and sat on the edge of the bed, motioning for her to join him.

Shannon slipped next to her husband. "She asked us to locate you."

Jayden audibly sighed through his nose. "She's dying, man. And she wants to see you before she goes."

Manny blinked and shook his head. "I have nothing to say to her."

"Well, evidently she has something to say to you." Jayden's tone took on one of authority. Shannon inwardly pumped her fist. Great shot to the heart, hubby.

The man shot him a narrow-eyed expression.

Jayden raised his hands, palms up. "Hey, we aren't here to mess in your business, okay? Just delivering the message. The wife has her phone number. You could at least call."

The nephew sat down at the table. "It's been forty years since I last spoke with her. What would I say?"

"'Hello' works." Jayden scrunched his lips to one side.

Manny's eyes flashed fire, then his anger smoldered

into a nervous laugh. "Guess I could do that." He sat further back in the chair, his hands on his knees. "What time is it in Texas?"

Jayden glanced at the alarm clock on the bedside table. "They're an hour behind, so about eight-fifteen."

Shannon reached across the bed and lifted her cell phone from the side table. She waved it at their guest.

He stared at it as if trying to decide if touching it would scorch his fingers. He blinked and shook his head. "I've got my own. Write down the number and I'll call her."

"Okay." Jayden motioned to Shannon, who punched up her password.

She scrolled through the contacts. "Here it is. Shall I text it to you?"

"No." His response came out quick and sharp. It made Shannon jolt.

His face softened slightly. "Just give it to me. I have a good memory."

She swallowed as she shifted her eyes from him to Jayden. Her husband's face held a go-ahead expression. "Very well. It's 210-555-5257."

He scoffed. "5257? That's my birthday." His mouth twitched.

"Hardly a coincidence, if you ask me." Jayden folded his arms, his voice low and stern.

"Whatever." The guy rose.

Shannon wanted to slap the man. She balled her fist and stared at Jayden.

Jayden broke eye contact with her and got up as well.

Manny sauntered to the door and jerked it open. He responded without turning his salt and peppered head back to their faces. "Thanks for delivering the message."

He shut the door behind him with a wham.

Jayden stood glued to the spot watching as if he half expected the dude to return.

Shannon plopped onto her back, feeling the mattress hug her like a matronly babysitter trying to calm her. But her breaths came short and frequent. "Of all the nerve. What an ungrateful twerp. He acted like a three-year-old being forced to eat Brussel sprouts."

Jayden snickered. "A lot of hurt lies in those years. On both sides."

"Do you think he'll call?"

"Maybe." He eased next to her and drew her to his chest. "Wanna pray about it?"

Emotion constricted her throat. "Yeah. I do." She pressed her forehead into his chest.

The conviction of his words and the strength of his arms encasing her melted her into a warm goo of protoplasm. Mrs. P. was right. Jayden Johnson was a good man. Her man. She silently thanked God for bringing him into her life, even if it often felt as if he wasn't.

A thumping on their door woke Shannon. She gasped and drew the covers to her chin. Jayden groaned, threw back the blanket, and stared at the digital clock. "What on earth? It's barely seven in the morning."

He rose and peered through the peephole. With a sigh, he unbolted the security lock and edged it open large enough for his face to be revealed.

"Yeah, what is it now, man?"

Manny's voice sounded from the other side, higher-pitched and determined. "I want to know more about my aunt."

"Hold on." Jayden rubbed the back of his neck. "Meet us at the breakfast buffet in fifteen minutes. We'll talk then."

Not waiting for a response, Jayden closed the door and re-bolted it. He blew a long breath out of his mouth and stomped to the bathroom. He muttered as he passed by the bed. "The man has some nerve. You can come or stay here. Your choice."

"I'll come." Shannon slipped out of the covers and began to gather her things.

"Okay. Let me get a quick shower then it's all yours.

Can you start the coffee pot?"

He slammed the door to the tub area.

"Sure." She responded to the wood between them and grabbed the small pot to fill it from the sink's tap. His irritation seeped into her. She checked herself. It wasn't aimed at her at but the whole situation and the demeanor of the man who now waited outside. So much for a leisurely time waking up in each other's arms.

As the coffee pot gurgled and groaned as if it, too, hated to come to life, she combed her hair before digging in her duffel for her deodorant and fresh clothes.

The knobs on the shower squeaked. Jayden emerged in a towel, a blast of steam following him. He pecked her neck. "Your turn. Thanks for making the coffee."

She breathed in the fresh scent of hotel soap emitting from his body and a small urge tickled her lower abdomen. Her grouchy mood melted, and she reached up on tiptoe to peck his lips. "You're a good man. Jayden Johnson."

He grunted. "I'm trying. But right now . . ." His head jerked toward the front door of the motel room. "It's hard to be civil."

She gave him a sympathetic eye roll and went to take her shower.

Fifteen minutes later, they strolled together toward the lobby. Manny Andersen sat at a bistro table for four hugging a ceramic mug. Déjà vu. He looked eerily like

Mrs. Perkins had last Sunday in the café. Had it really only been a few days ago?

He noticed their arrival and nodded in their direction.

"Let's get some food first. Make him wait a bit more." Jayden headed for the buffet line. Shannon followed though her stomach objected. She chose a bagel, a packet of strawberry cream cheese, and a plastic cup of skim milk.

Jayden took his sweet time toasting two Belgian waffles while he grabbed a banana, three pats of butter and two packets of syrup, along with another cup of coffee.

She waited for him, holding her condensation-dripping cup of milk in one hand as she balanced the plastic plate of bagel in the other. *Come on, hon. I don't want to sit down without you.*

As if he heard her thoughts, he plopped the heated waffles on his plate and eased with a confident strut toward her and their waiting guest. Jayden set his food down and pulled out a chair for her. She slipped into it and began opening her cream cheese tub.

He shook two sugars into his coffee, hardly acknowledging the man sitting with them.

The whole time, Manny's eyes shifted between them. His finger tapped the side of his mug.

Jayden took a sip, grimaced, and reached for another packet of sugar. "Okay. You woke us up. Now tell us why the change of heart." He clanked the spoon around the rim as his eyes bore into Manny's forehead.

The man's Adam's apple wobbled. He glanced around the room then down at his own coffee. "There is something you need to know."

"Okay?" Jayden leaned back into the spindles of the chair.

Their guest's eyes darted between them again. He nodded, seemingly to convince himself to speak up, judging by the puckered expression on his face. After a minute, he peered into Jayden's eyes as he leaned over the small table. He spoke in a low voice. "I gotta come clean, man. I'm not Manny Andersen."

Leaf Me Alone

Chapter Sixteen

Shannon choked on her milk. The room imploded around her and everything stood still. Had she heard him correctly?

"Say what?" Jayden now stood. His hand grasped the man's shirt. "What are you trying to pull?"

The room became dead silent, and Shannon noticed everyone staring at them. Well, to be fair, at that time of the morning it meant the two other people in the breakfast bar area and one waiter.

The man raised his hands. "Hear me out. I . . . I didn't know."

Jayden released him with a jerk and sat back down. "You have five minutes before I call 9-1-1."

Shannon's hand went to her throat. Part of her brain didn't want to believe what her eyes sent to it. Bob Martin had obviously sent him over to their hotel the night before.

Did he know as well?

As if to answer her question, the guy shook his head. "No one knows. I switched identities with him six years ago."

"How?" Jayden edged his torso forward over the width of the table, invading the older man's space. His elbows locked as he pressed his hands to the table.

The man blanched.

Shannon sucked in her breath. She'd rarely seen her cool-headed man get so irritated.

"I'll tell ya." Manny, or whoever he was, put his hands up in surrender.

Jayden sat back down.

"We were on the streets together off and on for years. At night, huddled in an alley behind a dumpster, or in a shelter if we lucked out, we'd talk, ya know? I guess we became friends." Pain washed over his features. He rocked his head from side to side as if to ease the tension in his neck.

Shannon blinked, still trying to make his words comprehensible. If he wasn't Manny, then who was he?

Jayden's muscles in his arms loosened. "Where is he?"

The man moved his head back and forth slowly. "I have no idea. I think he's dead."

"Dead?!" Shannon gasped.

Jayden's hand reached for her forearm as if to steady

her. "Start from the beginning. What's your real name?"

"Ernie. It's Ernie." He ran one hand over his whitened locks. "I got hooked on dope when I was a teenager. For a while, I could hold a job, but eventually, it took over my life. It jumbled up everything in here." He waved his hand in a tight circle over his head. "By my thirties, I ended up on the street with a few clothes in a plastic grocery bag. My girlfriend left it on the stoop when she moved out. Took our kid with her." He cocked his head as if apologizing.

Shannon pressed her lips together. Could she believe him? Or did he try to con them? She glanced at Jayden's face to try and read his reaction. His eyes focused on the man, but they narrowed like a snake's ready to pounce. She almost heard him hiss.

Ernie shifted in his chair. "I checked myself into a program and got clean. Then I tried to find her. And a job. I didn't succeed at either one." He wiped his hand down his face. "After a few years, I gave up. I ran dope for some guys to make money. Begged on the corners. You know, cardboard sign and all."

If Ernie tried to gain any sympathy with her man, it didn't work at all. Jayden raised his chin, his tone of voice flat. "Go on."

"That's when I met Manny. Ya gotta understand. Street people form a sort of community, but we are wary of each other as well. After a while you learn to trust nobody.

You compete for pocket change and a night in a shelter where you can get a meal and a shower. You watch your back. Keep your secrets close. We all have 'em."

He took a long sip from his mug and set it back down, wiping his lips on his sleeve. "After a while, we began to open up to each other. We'd both served. Me in the Army, he in the Navy. Both of our women left us and took our sons with them. We'd both tried to make a clean break and ended right back in the gutter. Several times."

Jayden's nostrils flared as he flipped his fork back and forth. Shannon could tell he became impatient. She slipped her hand into his and squeezed it.

He glanced at her and took a long breath before returning his attention to the man across from them. "So, how did you trade places?"

"That winter became brutal. It doesn't freeze much in Florida but that year it did. A lot. None of us had the clothes for it. Soup kitchens made extra meals and some church groups handed out hot coffee and blankets now and then. Manny developed a really bad cough. I led him to a place in an alleyway behind a dry cleaner. They run their machines at night, so the heat comes out the vents. Smells nice, too. We huddled there. He told me his son, who was grown by then and married, had found him and would put a hundred dollars in tens and fives in a post office box every month on the fifteenth. I think Manny knew he wasn't gonna need it anymore. He handed me the key and his wallet.

"At first, I didn't want to take it, but he insisted. We sort of looked alike. Same build and height. Same age. We were born ten days apart, isn't that something?" He shook his head. "Maybe fate. I don't know. Anyway, he told me to do it. Showed me how he stashed it in the hem of his pants. Tens in one leg. The fives in the other, all folded flat in strips. It was the end of the month, so he still had a few. He handed them to me. Then he curled up and went to sleep. Hacked all night long. Poor guy."

Ernie stopped and gazed at Shannon, and then at Jayden who'd decided to eat his breakfast while the man talked. Did that mean he'd calmed down a bit, or that he didn't believe a word this dude spouted and had shut him out? Shannon wasn't sure. But she doubted her bagel would get past her throat if she took a bite of it.

"I didn't know what to do. About sunrise, his breathing got really labored and wheezy. I gave him my blanket and snuck off. I flagged down two cops, told them where to find him, and walked away. The next two days, I hung out at the county hospital trying to find out what happened to him. For the next several weeks, I wandered in and out of shelters and the makeshift tents where the homeless congregate. I never found him. On the fifteenth, I went to the post office. He never showed. So, I used the key and opened the box. There sat the envelope. All it had on it was his first name. Inside, a hundred bucks, just as he said."

"I saw it as my second chance. I checked into the hospital again, got sober, and ended up with Bob Martin. I told him I was Manny Andersen and knew enough of his story to make it my own."

"Didn't Bob get wise to you? He struck me as a pretty savvy guy." Jayden's eyebrow arched.

"No. I told him I'd forgotten my social security number. He believed me. When the drugs and booze have rattled your brain for decades, some things fade. He applied for me to get a new one, as Manuel Andersen of course. I told him I was in the Navy and gave him my, I mean Manny's, birthdate and rank and age. He found a match. After that, I started getting government checks, most of which went to my upkeep at A Better Life. Eventually, I got my driver's license. Now to everyone, including the state of Florida, I am Manuel Parker Andersen."

Shannon's breath caught in her throat.

"Yeah, he named his son Parker. Family name on his mother's side. That's what he told me. His aunt is Grace Marie Parker Perkins. He told me about her, too. He regretted leaving her like he did, but he had been a very angry kid. His wife tried to get him to go see her. He refused to do it. His pride wouldn't let him. But, having her name in his always reminded him of her kindness, though he never deserved it. Then, when he was down and out, no way could he let his aunt know how he'd turned out, ya know?"

Jayden nodded. "I guess you never got back in touch with your kin either?"

Ernie didn't respond. He rubbed his thumb over the coffee mug. "I'm gonna get some more, okay?"

Jayden swished his hand, fingers pointing to the carafes like a king dismissing a servant.

Shannon waited until she figured Ernie walked out of earshot. "Do you believe him?"

His jaw remained stone-like, but his eyes softened as he looked into hers. "I am inclined to. It makes sense. Why else would he bang on our door at this ungodly hour?"

"To get us to back off. Go home." She shuddered. "I don't know, hon. Something about this is not right."

"I don't have your woman's intuition, but I have learned it is fairly trustworthy." He leaned to brush his lips on her cheek. "Let's hear him out. Then we'll see."

"All right. I guess." She scraped some cream cheese on her bagel and bit into it, though she didn't know why. The more she chewed the larger the lump grew in her mouth and the less her stomach wanted it.

Ernie returned with steam rising from his mug. He set it down without tasting it. "I did tell Bob about the money from Parker. I asked him not to contact Parker until I became clean and back on my feet. For my own intentions, I admit. It was easy money and more than I'd seen a long time. Bob insisted that I give him the key and that afternoon he returned with three envelopes from the past three months. He took one to cover my expenses and put the other two in his safe for protection. Every month we went together. I'd give him half and he'd put the other half in the safe. Did that for about two years and built up a nice nest egg of $1,500, but then Bob hired me on as staff and I made some good dough, so I began to leave another hundred in the envelope and not take any. I think Manny would have done that, too."

He reached into his pocket. "After three months of that, the envelope no longer contained money. Only this." He unfolded a piece of paper, smoothed the creases, and slid it across to Jayden and Shannon.

Shannon read it out loud. "Dad. It looks like you are back on your feet. That's good to know. I have been praying for that day to come. Here is my address if you ever want to get in touch. I won't tell Mom, promise. Love, Parker."

Ernie folded his hands. "Obviously I couldn't go through with that. I mean Parker probably wouldn't know the difference, but his mother might have."

Jayden stared at him. Shannon finally swallowed the bagel bite and remained quiet for once in her life, which surprised her. But this scene felt way too surreal, like a nightmare.

The man tapped the table. "Now you two come along." He lifted his hands in surrender. "I don't know anymore. I honestly don't."

He pushed back the chair and rose to leave.

Jayden grabbed his sleeve. "Wait, man. We aren't here to unravel your world. Let's think this out."

What? Shannon looked at her husband trying to figure him out.

Ernie stared into Jayden's face, too.

Jayden gazed back at him. Neither moved a muscle for a long moment.

Observing them reminded Shannon of those nature films when two rams meet in a glen. Except these two were not snorting at each other . . . yet.

Jerking his arm away, Ernie sat back down. "I don't want anything from the lady, okay? I just want to keep my job. And my apartment. I have a truck, too, but, well you know that."

"Yeah, man. We do." Jayden scoffed and shoved some waffle into his mouth.

"Sorry about that. When I drove into work and saw you, well, I wanted to figure out who you were and why you were in the van. I thought perhaps my cover had been blown. I guess I sort of knew the day would come, but . . ."

He raised his eyebrows into his forehead. "Last night, I went to ask Bob and he told me who you were. After I left your room, I drove around most of the night. Finally, at daybreak, as I watched the sun begin to rise, I recalled some scripture. The truth will set you free, or something like that. Maybe God was telling me something." He picked at the cuticle on his thumb for a moment then raised his gaze again to meet their eyes. "So, I decided to let the truth come out. I'm sorry I banged on your door so early, but I had to do it before I chickened out."

Shannon still didn't know how to respond. She peered into his eyes, seeing if she detected any truth in them. Part of her pitied the guy, but a larger part warned her not to get sucked into his story.

He worked his jaw. "Now that you know, what do you plan to do?"

Jayden rubbed a hand down his chin and shifted his attention to Shannon.

Shannon returned his glance. "Ernie, we'll be right back."

Jayden stood and pulled out her chair. She walked to the corner of the room, half-hidden by potted plants, away from most of the breakfast crowd.

He cocked his head when she stopped and turned back to face him. "Well, girl?"

Shannon wet her lips. "My woman's intuition radar is

on the blink all of a sudden, hon. You tell me. What should we do?"

"What would Mrs. Perkins suggest?"

"Prayer."

A grin slipped over his face. "Then let's do that." He tucked her fingers into his and pressed his brow against her forehead.

Leaf Me Alone

Chapter Seventeen

Ernie waited for them, which sort of shocked Shannon. They'd prayed together for at least five minutes, maybe more. She thought he'd see it as an opportunity to skedaddle. But he didn't.

When they returned to the table, he folded his arms across his chest. "Well? Did God give you any revelation?"

Shannon almost opened her mouth to verbally slap the cocky tone off his lips, but she checked herself. Suddenly, gazing into the man's face, she felt her anger slide off her shoulders into the cheap hotel carpet. She glanced down, as if expecting to find it again but instead studied the purple, tan and russet-colored swirls. Who picked these colors and patterns anyway?

Jayden cleared his throat. She glanced up and shook her thoughts back in place. But instead of irritation, only empathy settled over her. Not the emotion she expected at all.

Jayden seated her and then himself. His face remained stone cold yet calm like a cutthroat attorney who knew he had the jury in the palm of his hand. "No, nothing like a chorus from heaven or stone tablets."

Ernie snickered. "But one of the commandments on those said not to lie, right?"

"Or covet another man's things."

Ernie held up two fingers. "Okay. So that's two. I guess we could add stealing to the list."

His sudden contriteness melted her heart. Or had the prayer kicked into her soul? Maybe she had him figured wrong. Shannon decided to enter the conversation. "You say Manny gave you his permission to assume his identity. Then you accepted that gift. You were wrong to lie about who you were all these years, but if what you tell us is true you were fulfilling his last wish. He cared enough about you to want to see you have a better life." She realized that she'd just named Bob's facility and stopped, suddenly embarrassed.

A twinkle glistened in Ernie's eyes. "Good choice of words."

"You know what I meant."

"I do, Shannon. And I thank you for your insight. That last night, in between fits of hacking coughs, Manny told me everything he could as if he schooled me on things I would need to know. I think he honestly wanted me to go on as him. Maybe that's just my own justification, but I don't think so."

Jayden cleared his throat. "Then let's go with that. What would happen if you 'fessed up?"

Ernie shrugged. "I'd go to jail?"

"Probably." Her husband scoffed. "Tax fraud, fake identity. I don't think the state of Florida would take kindly to it."

He bowed his head. "I agree, Jayden. But that doesn't excuse my actions. I've duped a lot of folks, including myself for a while."

Jayden played with the last bites of waffle on his plate. "You've put us in a precarious situation. You get that?"

"I do." Ernie shifted his glance to Shannon. "Can you tell me about Mrs. Perkins?"

She gave him a soft smile as her mentor's face came to the forefront of her mind. "She is the most amazing woman I have ever met. Her faith is rock solid. Unshakeable. She's smart, too. And very intuitive. I think even in a medicated haze, she'd know you were not her Manny."

"You must think a lot of her to come all this way and try and track me, er Manny, down."

Shannon's insides warmed. "I do. I can't say she has changed my life, but she's sweetened it. Her faith and loving character have helped me become a better person." She shifted her attention to Jayden. "And I hope a better wife."

Her husband's eyes swam. He swallowed and caressed her fingers. "You do fine, girl."

For a moment their eyes locked. The "I'm sorry" that Shannon found so hard to express wrapped itself around her thoughts. Jayden bent to her ear. "It encourages me to be a better husband."

Shannon's cheeks heated and she knew it. She pressed her hands to them and swallowed the last of her now room-temperature milk.

Jayden pulled away and returned his attention to the man sitting across from them. "Ernie, if you came clean, I know Bob would do everything in his power to give you a good word. Shannon met a state social worker on the bus coming here who said he would help in any way to find Manny. He has a lot of influence from what I gather. I think you could rely on him, too."

The man's chest heaved as if a heavy weight had been lifted from it. "I'm tired of living a lie. Will you two really help me?"

Jayden extended his hand. "If you help us find out whatever happened to the real Manny Andersen."

Ernie hesitated to take it. "How?"

"You have connections of your own, even after this

long of a time. If anyone can locate him, it's you."

"But I failed before." His eyes shot between them as the sides of his eyebrows drooped.

"No, Ernie. You gave up. You decided to take the gift and walk away." Jayden sharpened his focus on the man.

First, a flare of anger flickered, then acknowledgment seeped into Ernie's face. He rubbed his chin but didn't look either of them in the face. "Yeah, guess so."

Jayden sat back, his arms crossed. Point made.

Shannon released her breath. Jayden had a way of cutting through the garbage to the truth. She always admired him for it. But the man might now shut down before they got any more info from him. She addressed Ernie. "Don't you think that if Manny had recovered, he'd have wanted the hundred dollars a month from Parker? He'd have found you again. I know in my heart of hearts he didn't survive long after that night."

Jayden's eyes drew together. He gazed at Ernie, then Shannon, and then back to Ernie. "I have a wise wife, don't I?"

Ernie nodded. "Yeah. You do, man."

"Do you recall the exact date it all happened?" Shannon grabbed her phone from her purse.

"Oddly enough, yes. May 12, 2012. My real fifty-fifth birthday. I'd always told myself that would be when I planned to retire. I guess in a way, I did." He harrumphed, but his face drooped further. His lower lip quivered.

"Ernie, what did you do with the $1,500?" Jayden changed the subject, Shannon figured in order to help keep the man from breaking down in front of strangers.

"Put a down payment on my apartment and then on the truck."

"Then it was money well spent. I'll make you a deal. You come clean to Parker Andersen and Bob Martin. Then the three of you can discuss if you should continue Manny Andersen's legacy or not. That is not for Shannon or me to decide." He reached in his wallet. "But here is my card. If you change your mind about coming to Texas and meeting Mrs. Perkins, let me know. We'll be here the rest of the day and leave in the morning."

Ernie extended his hand first this time. Jayden shook it firmly.

Shannon smiled. "Here is the business card of my new friend at the state that Jayden mentioned. I think he would be a great resource for you."

Most of the anxiety that had been building under Ernie's cheeks released with an elongated sigh. "I don't know how to thank you. It seems God keeps giving me a break, and I don't know what I've done to deserve it."

Jayden winked. "I never took one of Grace Parker Perkins' courses, but I have a feeling she'd say none of us deserve His mercy or grace. He freely gives it out of love."

Shannon asked for Ernie's phone. He handed it to her, and she keyed in her phone number. Then she found the Bible verse app and loaded it for him. "Here. Start reading Philippians. It's Mrs. P.'s favorite. I think it will mean a lot to you. I'm no expert, but if you have any questions, text me."

He blushed. "I will. God bless you both."

They stood and hugged. Then they waved goodbye.

On the way back to their room, Shannon tucked her arm into her husband's. "Did we do the right thing?"

He playfully bumped her in the side. "Yeah. We did, and I believe Mrs. Perkins would agree." He chuckled. "I certainly didn't feel this way when we sat down. I was ready to deck the guy."

"I know."

"Funny how prayer changes things."

Shannon brushed her hand across his cheek. "Yeah." Swallowing back her emotions, she strolled with him back to their room.

But as if a fog had lifted, her mind began to take over as more and more questions floated to the surface.

Leaf Me Alone

Chapter Eighteen

As they walked back, Shannon kept sighing. Jayden knew that meant her brain churned in several directions. He pictured a minuscule elf inside her head flipping through files but unable to locate the right one. "What are you mulling over?"

"Doesn't the military fingerprint enlistees?"

"Yes, they do. When I served in the Army those three years before we met, they took mine. I'm sure the Navy does as well. That way, at the end of a bloody battle they can identify . . . oh, I see what you mean." He glanced at her. Smart woman. "Why didn't the coroner identify Manny as a veteran?"

"Exactly. If he had died that night, or soon after in a hospital from exposure or whatever, that would be the first thing they'd do. Right?"

Jayden waggled his head. "Possibly."

"And then there's dental records. They are more reliable than fingerprints. Surely the military has records of those. I mean he served, what? Over twelve years? He's bound to have had a cavity or something. How could we find out?"

"Maybe your bus friend, Matt, can answer your questions."

She snapped her fingers. "Or Chase might. He's a detective." She fished out her phone and began to text him.

A few minutes later he called. Shannon put him on speaker as she sat on the edge of the bed and motioned for Jayden to join her.

"Hey, Shannon. What's this you want to know about fingerprints?"

"Well, another former homeless person believes he met Manny Andersen when they were street buddies, but he thinks he died of exposure years ago." She cringed and cast a glance toward Jayden. She mouthed that she didn't know what else to say.

Jayden winked. He knew she didn't want to blow Ernie's cover or get him in trouble . . . yet. And he liked being a witness to her mind kicking in gear. The girl did have smarts.

Chase's voice came through the phone she held in her palm. "If so, he is probably buried in a municipal or county cemetery as a John Doe. Most of them are."

A pained expression washed over Shannon's face. "Yeah, but Chase, wouldn't they take fingerprints to try and discover who he was?"

Jayden tilted his head toward the phone speaker. "He had been arrested in a store robbery so they'd have a record, right?"

"Recently?"

"No, man. Back in 1988 or so. Right, hon?" Jayden shrugged at Shannon.

She nodded. "That's right. But he was released, and the charges dropped."

Chase's voice lowered. "Then you may be out of luck. There is no set amount of time for a law enforcement agency to keep fingerprints on file for suspects that were never convicted."

Shannon's face puckered with determination. Jayden knew the expression. She could be like a dog willing to dig up a whole backyard in order to find a bone. She raised the phone closer to her lips. "But on TV . . ."

Chase puffed a breath through the receiver. "I know, the detectives put the prints through a computer and *voila*. That's fiction, Shan. The FBI has that capability, but they only keep fingerprints for a certain time period after a *federal* criminal has been released back into society. And they are not the main depository for every law enforcement in the U.S. Each state, and sometimes counties, have their own database."

"He served over ten years in the Navy, though. They fingerprint, right?"

"When did he serve? I mean, you're looking for a guy in his sixties from what I understand from Bailey."

"True. Let me see." She flipped through her notes on her phone app. "Ah, here it is. 1975 until 1988 or so."

"Well, the military keeps longer records. But you're talking decades since he was discharged. I imagine they do a purge now and then. Besides, it's not like a coroner can send in a set and they put it in a database to find a match. From what I understand, the coroner must submit a name first and give the military a reason to conduct the search."

"What about dental records?"

"The coroner would keep a record of the dental work logged in the autopsy report in case someone eventually came forward for the remains. But that person would have to have obtained the records to match them. I mean you can't walk in and say you recall your uncle had four teeth on the upper right knocked out in a fight as a teenager."

Shannon's body drooped. "Oh, I see."

Jayden felt the urge to hold her. He hated to see his wife's bubble being popped.

"Shannon, the truth is local governments run on tax dollars, and often there just isn't enough to go around for massive research. Cold case files are a reality. After a while, the officials must empty the morgue of the unidentified bodies and dispose of them. Even a pine box costs hundreds of dollars. Sorry."

"That's okay, Chase. I appreciate the information. Really." Shannon repositioned herself. "One more question, though. Can a citizen inquire if the coroner had any John Doe cases six years ago around May 12?"

"Not without a legitimate reason and possibly a court order to investigate. You have no proof he is actually dead, do you?"

"No." Her mouth scrunched to one side as her face deflated like a two-day-old helium balloon. It tugged at Jayden's heart. He wished he could blink his eyes and have the answer magically appear on the hotel TV screen.

Shannon's fingers traced the stitching on the bedspread. "So, there is really no way to determine if Manny Andersen is dead or alive if he doesn't pay taxes, have a driver's license, or hasn't committed a crime in the past few years. That's what you are saying, Chase?"

"Afraid so, Shannon. Sorry. Many of these homeless people drift off the grid. Wish I had a different answer for you and for Mrs. Perkins. I know how much she means to y'all. Bailey seemed a bit concerned last night after visiting her."

"I know. Which brings up something else that has been on my mind."

Chase chuckled. "And that would be . . ."

Shannon sat up straighter. She stole a look at Jayden, but he knew she didn't ask permission. He held his breath. Here we go.

"Is there any way to find out if the death rate at the Golden Days Hospice Center is normal?"

"Excuse me?" Chase scoffed. "Um, Shannon. I'd assume it was a hundred percent. I mean, we are talking hospice."

"I know." Her enthusiasm waned again. "Never mind."

"Funny thing is Bailey asked me the same question this morning when we met for breakfast. And she'd hinted at it before. What are you two cooking up?"

"It just seems an awful lot of people have died since Mrs. Perkins was admitted."

"That's Bailey's spin, too. I really think you two are barking up the wrong tree. People go there to die in a humane, dignified manner. Is there any indication she is being mistreated?"

Her eyes lifted to the ceiling. "Well, no. Except she thinks someone is sneaking into her room at night and drugging her."

"They probably are. Pain levels soar at night. They'd give her a heavier dose of morphine to help her sleep, Shannon."

"I guess." Her exhaled sigh lasted a long time. She flopped back on the bed, still staring at the ceiling.

Jayden leaned back on one elbow and ran his finger down her arm.

"You three did uncover an unsolved crime in Bailey's family. I get that. And helped Jessica exonerate her late father. But it doesn't mean there is a mystery around every corner. Not every death is suspicious. Especially in a place like that."

She rolled her eyes and sat back up. "You're right. Sorry. Tell Bailey I'll be back in a few days."

"I will." Chase's tone of voice lifted. "Hey, Jayden, my friend. Take care. It was good to see you at the restaurant. Let me know when you are headed back this way, and if your wife will release you from her claws for a few hours, we'll go shoot some hoops."

Shannon's eyebrows pushed together. "Claws? Are you commenting on my manicure, Chase Montgomery?" But a grin spread across her cheeks that Jayden knew reflected in her voice.

Jayden laughed. "Don't go getting' me in trouble, man. But, yeah. Plan on it."

They hung up. Shannon laid the phone down between them, crossed her arms, and stared out the window.

He heard her sniffle. Not a good sign. "What do you want to do now?"

She swiped her cheek with a maroon-coated fingernail. "Find the pauper's cemetery."

"You believe he's dead, then."

"Maybe I'll be able to sense that for sure if I walk the graves."

Jayden didn't argue. He knew his wife had an uncanny intuition for things, and usually, they played out. If she needed to spend the day traipsing through a graveyard, so be it. He'd man up and accompany her, even though cemeteries sent prickles up his spine.

"Let's freshen up, and you can do a computer search."

She bobbed her head as a whispered okay pushed through her plump lips.

Later that morning, they slipped through the rusty iron gate into Sunland Cemetery. Each carried an armload of daisies. Jayden had stopped and bought a bucketful from a street vendor.

Many of the older graves were marked by numbered cement cylinders, some tilting because they'd sunk in the turf over time. Only a few had names on them.

"There." She pointed to three rows of metal poles, each with a numbered marker on it. "Those look newer."

They strolled closer, careful not to step on any flattened mounds. Jayden scanned up and down the rows.

"Do you have any idea where his might be?"

She shook her head and placed a flower by the first

pole. She continued down the row.

Silently Jayden followed, handing her his batch, one by one, when hers ran out. At the end of the third row, they looked back.

They'd bought enough to place one stem on each site.

Shannon took in a deep breath. "Not a coincidence."

Jayden side-hugged her as the reality of this scene flooded over him like steaming water from a showerhead. "No, hon. It's not. No one may know who these folks were, but God does. And today, through you, He showed He cares. I'm proud of you."

She reached up on tiptoe and brushed her lips against his cheek. "Thanks. Let's go get a bite to eat."

Then they both turned and strolled to the car, hand in hand.

Jayden felt empty inside. Shannon rarely failed at anything. In fact, he couldn't recall a time she didn't excel. In school an A- was a disappointment, a B meant travesty to her. She'd always assumed if a person worked hard, lived right, and loved others, then life would iron out the wrinkles along the way.

But now, the fact that she had not found Manny Andersen gnawed at her gut. He could see it in her face. And the fact she remained silent until they reached the restaurant.

Jayden opened the door for her. "You okay?"

"Yeah. My brain is numb. Maybe I'm hungry. I couldn't really eat that bagel at breakfast."

She forked through her fried rice as if searching for the answer. Maybe the fortune cookie the waiter had brought with their meal would hold a clue. He crushed it in his hand and the cellophane popped. He pulled out the small strip of paper.

She leaned in. "What does it say?"

"The answer never comes easy. Keep trying." He gave off a half-hearted chuckle.

She rolled her eyes and poked at a snow pea.

He had to cheer her up. Fix this somehow. "You tried your best, girl. No one can ask for more than that. If anything, then perhaps Mrs. Perkins can look forward to the reunion in heaven."

She huffed into her eyebrows. "If he headed in that direction. We don't know that either." She set her fork down with a clunk.

Jayden's hand reached for her. "My grandpa always told me that God never wants anyone to be lost. He will try up until the very last breath to grab someone's attention. If we can believe Ernie's story, Manny gave him a new chance at life that night. That says something."

"If we can believe?" Her words pricked his thoughts. "You think Ernie is lying, girl? That he found Manny dying or already dead and stole his identity? How would he know about the box at the post office and what it contained?"

"If a homeless person is carrying a key, it had to be important." Shannon pointed her fork at Jayden. "And post office keys are pretty unique looking."

"Look. Perhaps at first Ernie's motive was pure survival. Take what Manny no longer needed. But the fact is, somehow, he got into Bob Martin's program and it turned him around. That much I could believe."

She picked through her rice again and decided to take a bite. He liked his wife thin, but the girl hadn't eaten much since they arrived. Nibbled mostly.

As her mouth worked, he could sense she chewed on his comments as well. After a moment she mumbled through her food. "I guess. Do you think he will contact Parker and come clean?"

The same thought hit them both at once. "Parker!"

She pulled the address from her pocket, her face suddenly bright with hope. "Mrs. Perkins put money in that account for him all those years. Maybe he would want to meet her before she passes on. If we can't bring her Manny, we can bring her his son she never met."

Jayden's smile widened at her renewed enthusiasm. "I've got another twelve hours before I need to load up and head for Mississippi. Where does he live?"

"In Jacksonville."

Jayden pulled it up on his phone. "It's over two hours

east of here on the Atlantic coast, at the end of I-10. You don't suppose he drove across the state once a month to put that money in that box, do you?"

She cocked her head in that curious way that always tugged at his psyche. "Maybe he has business here in Tallahassee. Maybe he works for the state or something."

"Or hired someone to do it. This just gets weirder. So, what do we do? Go pound on his door?"

Shannon sat up straight, a sly twinkle in her eye. "No, we have his phone number."

"We do?"

She scrolled her phone contacts. "His wife, Beverley, phoned me. She gave me Martha Walter's phone number. Now if I can just remember which is which. They both start with 904."

"Way to go, girl." He pointed to her screen. "The one that called you. The other you called. See the arrows?"

She tapped her temple. "Duh. Thanks. What would I do without you?"

Her question stirred something his heart. He'd wanted to hear her say that for so very long, and now he realized it. And what he had to do to be around more as clearly as if it had been scrolled on the restaurant menu. He took her hand. "Seems you do fine most of the time, but I want to change that."

"Hon, I know you took the long haul because it's good

money. It's just that . . ." She rubbed her thumb over his knuckles. "It's hard sometimes."

"It's not easy on me, either, girl." He raised her hand to his lips. It felt warm. "What keeps me going is I know I have the most wonderful lady waiting for me at home. I am blessed. I'd never do anything to jeopardize that, girl. Never. I'm sorry this has taken a toll on us both."

Her lips quivered. The question he knew she never wanted to ask he'd just answered. Tears swam in her deep brown eyes as she whispered in his ear the words he never got tired of hearing. "I love you, hon."

He released her hand and stroked her hair. "I know. And I love you."

He suddenly felt as if the whole restaurant stared at them as if they were a sappy romance movie on TV. He cleared his throat. "Show me later. Right now, let's contact Parker and Beverley."

Mirth glistened in her face. "Yes, sir."

A giggle floated between them as she fanned her cheeks before tapping the call button.

Beverley answered with a question hanging in her hello.

"Hi, this is Shannon Johnson. We talked yesterday about Manny Andersen, your father-in-law?"

"Yes?" Her tone sounded harsh.

She hesitated.

Jayden narrowed his eyes. He got out a pen and wrote on the paper napkin for her to read. *Maybe Beverley was unaware of Parker's monthly gifts to his dad.*

Shannon glanced at it and nodded. "We, um, have uncovered some information about him. May I speak with your husband if he's home?"

The woman didn't respond for a moment. Shannon pressed her lips together and glanced at Jayden.

He scrunched his mouth to one side before raising his iced tea glass to take a sip. At last Beverley's voice sounded again.

"I don't think you'd have anything of importance for him."

Shannon sucked in her courage. "Beverley, I don't mean to sound rude but isn't that for him to decide?"

Jayden pumped his fist and mouthed the words, *you go, girl.*

She gave him a tentative smile. They both knew either she'd opened the door or given the woman a reason to slam it in her face, so to speak.

"Very well. I'll have him call you. He's out running an errand right now."

She hung up.

"Well? What do you think, girl?"

Shannon darkened her cell phone screen. "She said she would give him the message. He isn't there right now."

Jayden motioned for their waiter to bring the tab. "Then we wait. Want a to-go box?"

"No. Well, okay. Chinese restaurants always serve much more than I can eat."

Her phone remained silent the rest of the night. Not that Jayden minded. Well, almost. The times with her were golden moments stolen from reality, and he didn't really want them to be interrupted. But in the middle of the night, she stared at the ceiling. He rolled over. "What's wrong?"

"What if Beverley never gave her husband the message? What if she did and it had caused a row between them?"

"What if Ernie had lied about everything?" He sat up and stared at her face, softly illuminated by the hall light coming through the curtains.

"If only we had his fingerprints." She rose to meet his eyes. "Wait. We do. On the note from Parker. They can lift them from paper."

"But Chase said the state of Florida and the Navy probably didn't retain them on file after this long."

She flopped back on her back. "True."

Jayden thought . . . hard. There had to be a solution. Then it popped into his brain. "Would he be fingerprinted to work at the museum, though?"

She shook her head on the pillow. "No, no, no. The man who claimed to be Ernie had applied as Manny. What good would that do, even if we did somehow lift his prints from the paper, if that was even possible? We'd have to find Manny Andersen's prints first and then have them compared. But how, after all this time could it even be done? And who would we convince to do it?"

She had a point. Jayden swallowed. "I don't know, girl. I wish I did."

She slammed her hand into her pillow and rolled to the wall. Jayden turned his attention to the ceiling this time. They both basically told Ernie they wouldn't pursue his deception if he came clean to Bob Martin.

His brain began to whir as fast as a child's spin top. Wait, their condition also meant he'd agree to tell Parker Andersen the truth. Had either of them even given Ernie his phone number? No, because earlier Shannon had to figure out which one it was.

Blast it. Ernie had pulled a fast one. What a con artist. Arghhhh.

Jayden rustled her. "Shannon?"

She flipped toward him and rubbed his stubbly cheek. "We should go back to sleep."

He lifted her fingers from his face. "You just made that impossible. Besides, I think Ernie lied."

He sighed and threw back the covers. He padded to the sink, flicked on the light in the toilet area, and filled two glasses with water. When he brought them back to bed,

Shannon took the one he handed to her.

"Excuse me?"

He set his glass on the bedside table. "He promised he'd get in touch with Parker Andersen but didn't ask for his contact info."

"Which means?"

"He has no intention of contacting him."

"Where are you headed with this?" She swiveled around to face her husband. He could see the puzzlement in her eyes even in the darkened room. "What if Ernie was really Manny Andersen and made the whole thing up to stay anonymous?"

"But why would he do that?"

"To get us to leave him alone. He had second thoughts after he spoke with us the first time."

Shannon groaned and slid under the covers. "Oh, Jay. Your brain had to go there, huh?"

Leaf Me Alone

Chapter Nineteen

"Sorry."

Shannon rose and dug the take-out bag from the mini-fridge. Now she finally felt hungry though she didn't know why. She reheated the contents in the motel microwave and brought it over to the bed. As she took some in her mouth, she couldn't help but smack her lips. She dug the fork in for another mouthful.

Jayden paced as she ate. "That stuff stinks."

"Tastes good."

"Oh?" He reached over, grabbed her fork and shoveled a large amount into his own mouth.

"Hey."

He shrugged as he chewed and stuck the plastic utensil back in the pile of food. He plopped back on the bed, head propped on his hands.

"Okay. Run it by me again. I'm trying to wrap my

brain around what you said." She wiggled the black fork in his direction.

He repeated his thoughts. They made a lot of sense.

Wiping her mouth on the paper take-out napkin that smelled somewhere between pepper and bug spray, she nodded. "If you think about it, the whole story seems rather fanciful. Like something out of movie plot."

Jayden swallowed a chug of water. "So, you agree he is sending us on a wild goose chase?"

"Or red herring. Isn't that what they call it in the mystery books?" She shoveled the last bite into her mouth and broke open the fortune cookie she had never eaten.

As she read it, half of the rice returned to her throat. She felt her eyelids stretch toward her temples. Coughing, she waved it at her husband.

He grabbed it and held it up to the light streaming from the bathroom.

"To tell only half the truth is to give life to a new lie." He read it again silently, moving his lips. Then he shook his head. "No way."

Tingles zipped up and down her arms. "Jayden. What do we do now?"

He rose off the bed and flicked on the light. "Get dressed and find an all-night diner. You've made me hungry now. And neither of us can sleep after this revelation."

He stomped over to his clothes.

Shannon followed his instructions, ignoring the glow from the digital alarm clock that read 2:13 a.m. The whole time they dressed and drove to find a twenty-four-hour café, they batted the what-ifs back and forth.

"We need to speak with Bob Martin, girl. Tell him everything."

"But isn't that breaking our promise? You told Ernie it wasn't our business."

Jayden pulled into the diner's parking lot and killed the engine. "I guess I did."

"So, what do we do?"

"Order waffles and bacon. And cheesy scrambled eggs."

She huffed a breath. Always the clown. "I'm serious."

He jerked the car door open. "So am I. I need sustenance in order to get my brain in gear. And caffeine. Not that watery hotel garbage." He slid out of the car, then leaned back in toward her to finish his thought. "Besides, in about six hours we need to return this car to Bob anyway. The man's bound to ask us if we found out anything. We need to decide what to tell him."

"True." Shannon sighed. What a mess she'd gotten them into.

Over a hearty breakfast, they weighed their options. Could someone really pull off becoming another person? If anyone knew the answer it might be Bob Martin. They both imagined he saw practically every situation in his field of work. But to even broach the subject meant they would be going back on their word to Ernie.

"Maybe we need to track him down again and pump him for more information. Or agree to drive him to meet Parker."

He swallowed the last of his coffee, his eyes remaining on her face. He wanted her reaction? She'd give it to him. "Jayden. You must be on the road soon. I don't see how."

Her husband ran a hand through his hair. "I'm calling dispatch and telling them I can't do the haul."

Say what? Jayden Johnson never called in. Ever. Not even when he was ill. "No. You can't do that."

His eyes sharpened onto hers. "I can. This is important, girl. I am not letting you traipse around Florida on your own."

She opened her mouth to speak, but he put up his hand to stop her.

"And no, I don't want you calling Bailey or Jessica, or even Chase or Grady to come help. This is for you and me to handle. Let them handle Mrs. Perkins and the folks dropping like flies in that hospice center. And yes, that bugs me, too."

She clucked her tongue at his unintentional pun. Part of her wanted to throw her arms around him, but the other portion wanted to tell him he was nuts. "What will you say to dispatch?"

"I have a family issue I need to take care of. We get five days personal time off. I'm calling it in."

He lifted his cell phone from his back pocket and began to dial. When the dispatch answered, he rose and walked to the vestibule.

Shannon fisted her hands in her lap. She studied his face trying to decipher how this conversation went. But Jayden turned his head away.

She closed her eyes and sent up a prayer. Then she heard his footsteps returning.

"Well?"

He sat back down and took a long sip of his coffee. "They gave me an ultimatum. Finish the haul or turn in the rig to the warehouse in Orlando."

An icy grip grabbed her in the middle of her chest. "Meaning?"

"Meaning I play their game, or I walk. I told them I'd have the rig back in Orlando by noon today. They know where to send the pay they owe me."

A buzz filled her ears. Had he just been fired?

"Jayden, no."

He rubbed his thumb over her forearm. "Hon, if they can't grant a man time to take care of family, then they don't care enough about him. I don't want to work for folks like that."

"What are you going to do now?" Her pet and plant service made a nice hunk of change but not enough to meet all their expenses.

Jayden raised her hand to kiss it. "Help you find the truth. Then we'll see. I was looking for a job when I found this one, girl. Maybe it's time I came home for good. I miss you way too much, and spending this time together has convinced me I don't want to be away from you anymore."

Tears swam in the back of her eyes. "I'd like that. I've missed you. Do you think you can find work in San Antonio?"

He leaned back against the booth. "I can start a local home delivery service. It's the going thing now, you know. More and more of the national chain stores and restaurants are doing it. To compete, the local establishments are bound to need drivers. I could cut them a deal and build up a nice little business. Maybe have to hire helpers." He winked and shoved a wedge of egg into his mouth.

Oh, dearest Lord, guide us. Shannon's appetite disappeared into her coffee mug.

Bob Martin stared at them from his side of the desk.

His hands grasped the arms of his desk chair.

Shannon knew they had popped his bubble. They'd begun by thanking him for the use of the car, after filling the tank. Then Jayden casually inquired if Manny had been in contact with Bob the day before. When Bob revealed that he had not, that gave Jayden the opening to convey what had happened. She watched his face as her husband relayed the tale about Ernie becoming Manny. Bob's favorite success story. A lie. Her heart ached for him.

She laid a hand on Jayden's arm signaling him to stop for a minute and let all of this soak into the poor man's skull.

He stared at them, his fingers tented. Somewhere in the distance —from the parlor perhaps?— a clock ticked. At last, he sighed. "I'm floored, to be honest. I need a minute for this to sink in." He rapidly shook his head and got up from the desk. "Can I get you folks a soda or iced tea?"

Jayden's eyes moved to Shannon's. She gave him a quick head bob. "Sure. Anything diet for me. He takes the real stuff."

Bob chuckled. "Be right back."

As his footsteps faded down the hallway, Jayden let out a long sigh and rose to pace the room.

Shannon glanced at the posters, the items on the bookshelf and the stack of folders about to topple on the desk. She almost reached to straighten them, then decided against it.

Bob returned with a tray, containing three glasses of fizzy liquid and a bowl of roasted peanuts. He handed Shannon one. "Diet."

She thanked him, took the glass and held it in her lap with both hands. The cool condensation felt good on her sweating palms. But as she raised the glass to her lips, the tiny bubbles caught in her nose. She coughed.

Bob handed her a napkin. "Carbonation. Sorry, the can was not refrigerated when I poured it over the ice. The men usually don't go for anything that doesn't contain sugar."

She waved her hand over her mouth and nose.

Jayden crossed one leg over the other. "What's your gut feeling, Bob? Is Ernie telling the truth or spinning a yarn?"

Bob tented his fingers. "Haven't heard that phrase in a while. To tell you the truth, I'm baffled. I always consider myself a discerning fellow. Little gets by me and, believe me, some of these men try all sorts of things. To think that guy duped me for years . . ." He shuddered the idea away. "Frankly, it may be my pride getting in the way, but I don't buy it."

Shannon set her drink on the area rug by her chair. "You believe this man really is Manny, and he fabricated this story to get us to back off?"

Bob blew a long breath through his nose. He gripped the desk in front of him. "The Manny Andersen I know wouldn't do anything like that. I've always known him to be honest and above board. Or so I thought."

Bob opened the filing drawer on his side of the desk and pulled out a manila folder. He laid it open on his desk and flipped through the pages as if perhaps something he'd missed all these years would jump out at him.

Shannon searched Jayden's face. He glanced back with a blank expression. She reached down and took a sip of her drink. The bubbles had settled this time and the cold liquid felt good cascading over her tonsils. She noticed him take a long gulp of his as well.

Bob's chair squeaked as he scooted forward, returning her attention to him. He licked his thumb and scanned through a few more papers. "On the other hand, stealing from each other often occurs. Homeless folks learn to be opportunists. If one dies, usually his few possessions disappear before the coroner's wagon shows up. Perhaps back then . . ." His eyes darted over the pages.

They waited for him to find whatever he searched for.

He closed the file and stared at it. "Nothing jumps out at me from my initial assessment notes. I don't know. I honestly don't."

Shannon caught the perplexity in his face and felt even more sorry for him. "Well, there is one thing for sure.

Either this man is lying now, or he's been lying for years. Either way . . ." She lifted one shoulder to her ear.

"True." Bob raised his gaze. "Describe him to me. This man who appeared twice at your door."

"Why?" His question came at her from far leftfield. Not at all what she expected him to say.

Jayden nodded at her. "Go ahead, girl. You're better at that than I am."

"Well, all right." May as well appease the man. It's the least she could do after they had shattered his ego like a confetti egg cracked over his head. Shannon closed her eyes for a moment. "He's about six-foot, because Jayden is six-one, and he was almost as tall but not quite. He has grayish eyes. But that may be because he wore a green janitor's outfit. It had the museum's name on it and his name, Manny." She opened her eyes again.

Bob nodded. "Good. Go on."

"He looked to be in his early sixties with whitening hair. More white than light brown. Oh, and he had a scar at the edge of his left eyebrow. It angled toward his scalp."

Bob's voice echoed off the ceiling fan. "What? Did it look new?"

Shannon flew open her eyes to stare at a white-faced Bob. "No, not really. I mean it wasn't pink. It had a fine white line."

Bob's eyes lit. "A scar, but not a large pox mark?

You're sure?"

Her heart skipped. "Not that I recall. Jayden?" She turned to him for an answer. Any answer.

He protruded his lower lip and shook his head in slow motion.

Bob scooted forward in his chair. "Did he have his hair combed over it?"

"No, his hair was combed straight back."

"Aha." Bob jolted to his feet and pointed at them with his finger. "Whoever that was who came to your room was not the man I know as Manny." He perched his hip on the edge of the desk and bore his gaze into them. "Now we have to figure out why."

"How?" Shannon's head switched from her husband to Bob. Jayden's mouth remained open as if he was catching a snowflake on his tongue. Bob had a weird grin on his face. She felt as if she'd just zipped down the rabbit's hole with Alice into Wonderland.

Bob scratched his chin. "Well, I'm the only one in this room who can positively identify the man who claimed to be Manny Andersen when he checked into this place. I guess I better head over to the museum and confront him."

"If it's him." Jayden raised a finger to make his point. "I mean, could Ernie's story be partially true?"

Shannon spun in her chair toward her husband. None of this made sense. "What are you suggesting?"

Jayden swiveled toward her. "That Ernie might have run into Manny recently, not years ago like he stated. Maybe they never were friends and seeing each other again fueled an old argument. Ernie killed Manny six months ago, stole his truck, and applied for the job in his place. That's why the move to a new apartment all of a sudden without giving any notice. He admitted they resembled each other."

The room began to shrink. Shannon's breath wouldn't push out of her lungs.

Bob pressed a hand on Jayden's shoulder. "That would explain the reason his emails stopped. I hope you're wrong."

Chapter Twenty

Bailey sat across from Chase at the diner. He thought she'd be excited about getting tickets to the new play in town, but she acted distant for some reason. And she did little more than push her food around her plate. He finished his pancakes, paid, and he walked her to the car.

"Are you alright, Bailey? You seemed preoccupied today."

Bailey leaned against the car door. "I can't shake this feeling that Mrs. Perkins needs me." She rubbed her eyebrow. "I don't know. Maybe because the last time I visited her she seemed so upset. Well, understandably."

"Do you want to drop by and see her now? It is barely eight, though."

Her eyes took on a glimmer. "Could we? I think regular visiting hours start soon."

Chase's heart melted. It was his first Saturday off in a

month. Though he wanted to spend it only with her, how could he refuse? Besides, if it eased her mind, then perhaps she'd concentrate more on his company. He brushed a strand of hair off her cheek. "Sure, babe. Let's go."

Her lips curled upward as he opened the passenger door for her. That smile always lit up his world. He resisted the urge to press his mouth to hers as he leaned in and handed her the seatbelt strap.

They chatted about the matinee he'd gotten tickets for as they drove out to the hospice facility, but he still didn't see much excitement dancing in her eyes. Mrs. P. must really be on her mind. Or was it something else she hadn't told him?

Chase noticed she kept sliding her fingers over the safety restraint as it clung to her shoulder. Nervous? He hoped that didn't mean Mrs. Perkins had taken a turn for the worse and Bailey subconsciously became aware of the fact. He noticed women often sensed things like that, especially kind-hearted Bailey.

All seemed quiet and normal when they entered the lobby and moved through the double doors. A nurse nodded to them in recognition as they walked down the corridor that led to Mrs. Perkins's room. Chase lowered his lips to Bailey's ear. "Should we have brought flowers or something?"

"No." She laid her hand on his arm. "Her room looks

like an English garden already. A lot of people have dropped by or had the florist send bouquets."

"Ah." Well, he tried.

"Sweet thought, though." She reached up and brushed her lips to his cheek, sending a shiver through his system. Then she tapped on the door. "Mrs. Perkins? It's Bailey and Chase. Can we come in?"

Though a soft glow, probably from a lamp, showed through the mostly closed doorway, no response followed.

Bailey raised her voice a bit more. "Mrs. Perkins?"

"Maybe she is indisposed." He shrugged.

"You wait here. I'll slip in and check."

Chase stepped a few paces back as she slid her slender figure through the doorframe.

Then he heard the gasp. And a squeal.

Adrenaline pumped into his arms and legs. He thrust open the door just in time to catch Bailey as her knees buckled.

Mrs. Perkins lay in the bed, her mouth open and her eyes blank. Her face took on an ashen color and the IV machine had been turned off.

Bailey shuddered under his grip. "Is she . . ."

Chase led her to a side chair and pressed her gently into it as his own heart did jumping jacks inside his chest. Then he walked to the bedside and laid two fingers against the old woman's neck. He felt a very faint thump of a pulse.

"I think we're in time. Get the nurse."

Bailey sat wide-eyed, unable to move. Didn't she hear him?

He pressed the red call button. A ding, ding sounded at the open doorway as a flashing red glow reflected off the highly polished floor in the corridor.

A calm, soft voice answered immediately. "Do you need help?"

Chase leaned toward the speaker and yelled. "Crash cart. Now."

Within nanoseconds, the room filled with staff shouting orders, wheeling in equipment, and pulling back the covers.

Chase lifted Bailey out of the chair by her arms and guided her into the hall.

She whimpered, her lip quivering.

He drew her to him, rubbing small circles on her back as she buried her head in his chest. Could she feel his heart ripping in two?

Lord, please don't let Mrs. P. go to you before Shannon and Jayden find Manny.

Bob pulled back his sleeve. "Okay, assuming he works

weekends, we have eight hours before he comes on duty. What do you want to do before then?"

Jayden's eyebrow arched, a sure sign of disgust or doubt. Shannon had seen it a few times when people fabricated a story. Had Ernie? It seemed that way.

With a scoff, he lifted his chin. "I bet he's already bolted. Maybe he's figured out by now we might be on to him since he hasn't contacted you. I'd sure as heck head out of town if I were Ernie."

Bob's shoulders slumped. "You may be correct, Jayden. But perhaps I could talk to the manager and get his description."

Shannon sat forward. "We could go back to his old complex and ask people there to describe who they knew as Manny. If it matches your description, then we'd know he was still alive six months or so ago."

Bob snapped his fingers. "Good idea."

Jayden swiveled to his wife. "I married a smart one."

Shannon dashed her gaze to her hands as she felt her cheeks rise in temperature.

The director scooted past them. "Yep. You did. Listen, I need to tell my assistant, Mark, I'll be out of pocket a few hours. Be right back."

Jayden's large hand reached for hers. "We'll get to the bottom of this."

She appreciated his support and his optimism. "It

seems our goal is slipping further and further away. What a mess."

"Don't give up hope, yet. There is another scenario."

"What?"

"Manny paid Ernie to put on this act."

Wow. She hadn't thought of that. "Why?"

"To get us to stop snooping into his life. He has no desire to see his aunt but didn't have the gumption to come forward and say so since he learned she's dying."

Shannon searched his face to determine if he believed what he'd just said or only tried to appease her. His jaw remained loose as he stared directly into her eyes. But she could almost see his brain cells in fifth gear. "Okay. Maybe so. If that's the case, they are probably both long gone, and our search has reached a dead end."

Jayden crossed a leg over his knee and weaved his arms into a pretzel pattern. "I wonder if there is any way to put a—what do they call it? — a BOLO out?"

"Be-on-the-lookout. Yes. I learned that from Chase. But we have no proof a crime has been committed, so I doubt the Tallahassee police would cooperate."

"No, they probably wouldn't." Bob's voice at the doorjamb made them both turn around.

"Sorry. I heard your conversation. Or part of it. Unless he has changed, the contrite and honest Manny I knew wouldn't concoct such a scheme to fool you two. He'd come forward and tell you face to face he didn't care to go to Texas." Bob came around the desk and reached in the drawer. "As I recall, he had quite a bit of remorse about the way they'd lost contact. My guess is he would see it as a blessing from heaven to be with her one more time and make amends." He pulled out a set of car keys. "This time, we take my car. I gather you two have had breakfast?"

"Yeah, we did." Jayden let out a scoff as his eyes angled to Shannon. "She couldn't sleep so we hit an all-night diner."

Bob smirked but his eyes held empathy. Shannon appreciated it. She marveled how the man could not be hardened after dealing with men who had been down on their luck for so long. She doubted if she could do his job. But then again, God hadn't given her the passion to do it as He obviously had given Bob.

Bob knew a shortcut to the old complex. They arrived within minutes. He pulled into the six-car lot and honked his horn. A woman, who had been bent over a flower bed, stood and waved as she removed her gardening gloves.

"Hi, Mabel. Those pansies are exceptional. You sure have a green thumb." He got out of the car.

Shannon shook her head. The man knew everyone.

Jayden slid out of the passenger seat and opened the back door for her.

The woman swatted the air in humility. "Long time no

see. What brings you by, Bob? These aren't new tenants I hope because we are all full up at the moment."

Shannon bit her lip to keep from uttering a snarky reply.

Jayden laced her hand in his. Out of the corner of his mouth, he commented to her in a whisper. "It would be a fair assumption, girl. Especially since Bob drove us here."

"I guess." She jerked her hand from his and walked in the direction of the woman who now shielded her eyes from the morning rays.

"These folks are looking for Manny. They are friends of his aunt and want to take him back to Texas to see her before she passes."

The woman's mouth opened in an O. "You're the ones who left the note, right? We spoke on the phone."

"Yes, ma'am." Shannon extended her hand. "We are Jayden and Shannon Johnson."

The woman wiped her palm on her pant leg and then took it in a firm grasp. "Mabel Adams. Nice to meet you. But as I said, Manny moved out about six months ago."

Bob propped one foot on the curb. "Mabel, you were here when he moved in, right?"

Psshh. A sound resembling air releasing from a bicycle tire came from her lips. "Now Bob, you know I have been the onsite manager for going on fifteen years. Yes, I was here. Signed the rental papers."

He nodded and pushed off, then evened his stance. "Humor me. I'll explain in a minute. Do you recall any distinguishing thing about his face?"

"You mean that huge pox mark on his temple. The one he always tried to hide in a comb-over?"

Bob shot a glance at Shannon and then Jayden.

"Did he have a scar near his eyebrow? Here?" Shannon motioned to the outer edge of her own on the left-hand side.

The woman pouted. "Not when he lived here, no."

Jayden puffed a long breath through his cheeks and rubbed his neck.

"What's this all about, Bob?"

"Well, Mabel, it seems the man who told them he was Manny isn't him at all. Then he fessed up to that and told them he took Manny's place over five years ago."

"What? But Manny moved out a little over six months ago." She shifted her gaze from face to face in confusion.

Jayden spoke up. "Exactly. He told us Manny was a homeless man and was dying from exposure, so he gave him his identity. He said he was the one who entered Bob's program pretending to be Manny."

She jerked her head back as if surprised. "And you say he had a scar on his eyebrow? No way he was the same man I knew, then."

Bob laid a hand on her shoulder. "That's what I told

them. So, you are absolutely sure Manny moved out and not someone who might have impersonated him."

"I sure am." She gave them a firm head nod. "It was windy that day and he kept pulling his bangs over that mark on his temple even though he knew I'd seen it a hundred times. Habit, I guess. It was huge, about the size of a dime."

Shannon turned to Jayden. "We would have noticed it, then, right?"

"Well, we were inside most of the time, but since you detected the scar just past his eyebrow, I'd think you'd have seen it as well. And, Mrs. Adams, you say the Manny you know had no such scar."

"You heard right, young man."

Bob extended his hand. "Thanks, Mabel. It was great to see you again."

She took it in both of hers. "Likewise. If I get a vacancy, I'll let you know."

"Please do. I will probably have two discharging from the program in a few months. They'll need a place to live."

She cackled as she patted his cheek. She turned to the Johnsons. "A saint straight from heaven, this one is. Been renting to him for going on seven years and never had an ounce of trouble from any of the men he sent over. Some still stay in touch."

Bob's eyes shone with pride. But Shannon sensed it was not in himself, but the men he'd helped. If she and

Jayden ever made some real money, she'd make a monthly donation to his cause.

They said their goodbyes and got back into the car. As Shannon and Jayden buckled in, Bob half turned so he could view both of them. "Well, folks. That answers one question. Ernie definitely spun you a yarn. Shall we head to the museum?"

Jayden turned to Shannon. "What do you think, girl? Or should we drive to Jacksonville like we talked about?"

"Jacksonville?" Bob asked it before Shannon could open her mouth.

Jayden shifted back toward him. "Yeah, we figure that if we can't find Manny, maybe we could bring his son, Parker, to meet his great aunt. She evidently put money in a small savings account for him when he was a kid."

"Really? Manny never told me." Bob scrunched his eyebrows together.

"He didn't know about it. When Parker graduated from high school, his mother, Manny's ex-wife, took him to Fort Meyers to withdraw it. It got him started into adulthood."

Bob shook his head. "Wow. This Mrs. Perkins must be one heck of a woman."

A lump formed in Shannon's throat. "She is."

Her cell phone chimed. "It's Bailey."

Bob mouthed the word, *who*.

"A mutual friend." Jayden motioned with his head. "They both know Mrs. P. Bailey is checking on her while Shannon is out here."

Shannon slid her finger across the screen to connect the call. "Hey, Bailey. What's . . . What?"

As Bailey's sniffly voice explained, the words echoed in her ear, not quite wanting to reach her brain. Tiny prickles skittered up her arms to her chest. "No. No." Tears sprung into her eyes and dribbled to her cheeks.

Jayden jumped out of the car and dashed to the back door. He pulled it open and enveloped her shoulders in his strong arm. "Hon?"

Shannon placed her hand over the phone, but it shook so much she almost dropped it. "Mrs. P." She swallowed. "Bailey and Chase found her unresponsive. They are working on her now to bring her back."

Saying the words glued the reality to her mind. She hiccupped and handed the phone to Jayden, not wishing to hear any more.

"Bailey, it's Jayden. What's going on?"

How could his voice sound so calm when hers screamed inside her head? Sniffing back tears, she bit her lip and watched as Jayden listened to Bailey's voice.

"Okay, I'll hold on." He placed his hand over the phone's speaker. "The doc's just come to speak with her and Chase."

Shannon grabbed his free hand. He drew it to him and squeezed her fingers.

In a few moments, Bailey came back on the line. Jayden listened, responding with a few "uh-huhs".

Shannon shook his arm to get his attention as Bob sat in the front seat, his face blank and his eyes wide open. When Jayden glanced in her direction, she mouthed the word *what*.

He bent his head toward her. "They've revived her. It's okay. But they are transporting her to the hospital for observation. She'll probably remain there for a few days."

A groan escaped from Shannon's gut, half out of relief and half out of residual shock over the news Bailey had conveyed. She didn't want to think time might run out before she could fulfill her promise. Or that Mrs. P. would die while Shannon was three states away, unable to tell her goodbye.

Jayden returned to the phone conversation. After a few more head nods, he spoke again. "Okay, girl. We're praying. Keep us posted. No, we've hit a snag. It seems we didn't find him after all. We'll call you later and explain. Say hi to Chase." He hung up.

"I'm glad he's there with her." Shannon's shoulders relaxed a bit. For the first time in minutes, she took an actual breath.

Bob cleared his throat. "Um, maybe you two should

head to Jacksonville as you planned. I can keep investigating here. Some of the men may still have street contacts. I also know a few cops I can call. If this Ernie is still in the area, we can track him down."

Jayden gave Shannon one more squeeze and released her as he addressed Bob. "Thing is, we can't believe Parker Andersen would drive all the way here once a month to put one hundred dollars cash in a locker."

"True, Jayden, unless he came here on business that often." Bob pointed his finger at them both. "But you can ask him that when you meet him. Let's not allow peripheral facts to muddy our focus."

Jayden sighed. "You're right, thanks."

He ran his hand down Shannon's afro as his eyes searched her face. His knitted brow told her he wanted to make sure she was okay before he returned to the front seat. She blinked that she was. He nodded and got out.

As he re-buckled his belt in the front seat, he motioned with his head toward Bob. "Okay. If you don't mind dropping us off at the motel, we'll check out and head that way. You have our numbers."

He tapped his finger on his phone, laying on the console between them. "I do. But please, take the Honda."

Jayden turned it down. "I've gotta return the rig to Orlando by tomorrow, so we'll take it instead."

Bob didn't ask why. Instead he turned over the

ignition.

Shannon watched the north Florida sunshine play through the leaves of the lush, tall trees as they drove by. The splotchy shadows and flickering light made the scenery surreal. Sort of the way her world felt right now. To think four days ago all she worried about was Fluffy eating a fizzy antacid. Now her husband was unemployed, her mentor lay at death's door, and a man who had been in their hotel room might be a murderer and knew how to get in touch with them.

She blinked back the residual dampness clinging to her eyelashes. *Lord, I know you have answers, and You will reveal them in Your timing. But we really need Your guidance right now. Tell us what to do.*

Leaf Me Alone

Chapter Twenty-one

Chase jiggled his leg, which meant he worked on a problem in his head. Bailey touched his shoulder. "Something is eating at you, isn't it?"

He huffed and stretched his legs out, crossing them at the ankles. The hospital waiting room hummed with various pitches of human talk mingled with the chatter of a news channel no one watched. The fluorescent lights added an eerie glow to the room, cloaking its occupants from any sense of real time.

"Why was her IV machine switched off? It doesn't make sense."

"I don't know. Maybe she only gets the meds and fluids a certain time of day. Not constantly."

He rubbed his hand over his mouth. "Perhaps."

She swiveled in the uncomfortable chair to face him. "You think something funny is going on there, don't you?

Shannon and I are right. People *are* prematurely dying in there."

"Whoa." He stopped her with his hand. "I won't go that far. If someone was smothering them with a pillow or something, then I'd say yeah, let's investigate it. But if someone is incompetent in administering their drugs, or not doing their job by checking their vital signs? Well, that's for a medical board to decide."

She shrugged. Maybe he was right. The doctor had told them Mrs. Perkins was no longer in danger. More than likely, she had experienced an overdose of the morphine building up in her system's fatty tissues and in her weakened state, the last scheduled dose had been too much for her body to handle. In elderly cancer patients, it was a common concern.

She decided to let it drop, for now. Her phone beeped. She keyed in her passcode and opened the screen. "It's from Shannon. She and Jayden are heading to Jacksonville to meet Manny's son, Parker. "

"Do they think he might be able to locate his dad?"

"Don't know. I'll find out." Her thumbs danced over the small keyboard. "No, but they want to see if *he* will come see Mrs. P. instead."

Chase straightened in his chair. "That means they've given up on the search for Manny?"

Now how would she know that? She swallowed the

snarky remark floating in her head. They were both on edge. Instead, she sucked in a long breath. "I'll call her and find out."

He nodded as if satisfied.

Shannon filled her in on what had happened as Jayden drove the rig cab across Florida.

"Unreal. Wow, Shan. That is creepy. So, you both think Manny was murdered?"

Chase sat up and frowned.

She pumped her hand telling him to wait a minute. She then rose and walked away with the phone pressed closer to her ear. The chatter of the TV news and the whiny baby crinkled her nerves. Out in the corridor, her friend's voice became stronger.

"We don't know. He may have paid the dude to play the part, but Bob doesn't think he'd do it. He says Manny acted remorseful about how he and his aunt had drifted apart all those years ago, mostly his fault. At that time, he didn't even know where she lived. I'm not sure what the truth is."

"So then, what's Bob going to do?"

"Put out feelers and see if anyone can locate this Ernie guy. He has a lot of street cred."

"Good. Keep me posted and we'll do the same at this end. God's got this, Shan. It'll work out." She said it as an affirmation to herself as well.

Bailey ended the call and wandered back to where Chase sat. When her eyes landed on him, her heart hitched. Again. He had revived in her what she assumed would always lay dormant after her fiancé died. Most of the time the emotions he stirred in her scared her, but right now it comforted her.

Thank goodness he had accompanied her to the hospice. What a way to spend his day off. Poor guy. She should bake him a thick, triple-layered chocolate cake with mocha icing.

She halted in mid-stride and rolled her eyes. Oh, great. A typical girlfriend response. Was that who she was now? Did he think it, too?

When he caught her coming toward him, his eyes softened. They told her, yes. He wanted her to be that. Maybe she should, then. It didn't sound half as scary as it had in the past. She eased into the chair next to him.

"Well?"

She gulped to relieve the dryness in her throat. She ran her fingers through his hair and smiled. "Chase. Thank you for being here with me. You have no idea how much it means to me. How much you mean to me."

His eyes lit as if someone had just flipped a switch. He cupped her chin and planted a soft, quick kiss on her lips.

The news anchor, crying tot, and everything else swirled into oblivion. She felt his arms encase her. She snuggled into his chest. It felt like home.

His voice vibrated as he rested his chin on her head. "So, what did Shannon say? Something about a murder?"

She laughed. Good gracious. The man oozed detective mode 24/7. No wonder he made chief at the age of thirty-five.

She raised up and patted his chest. "Let's go get some coffee and I'll explain. The noise level in here is getting to me."

"Sure." He rose and extended a hand to help her stand. With a soft smile, he wrapped one arm around her waist and shoved his other hand deep into his jeans pocket. With hips barely touching, they made their way to the cafeteria.

As people passed by, most of them smiled. She raised her gaze to see Chase sporting a Cheshire cat grin. She stopped and pulled him to the side, out of the pedestrian traffic. "Are you grinning like a tiger who just ate a gazelle for a reason? Is it because I let you kiss me or because I said the 'm' word, murder?"

He chuckled. "Both get my blood pumping, you know." Then he gave her the wink that always melted her resolve.

She playfully batted the air. "You're incorrigible. Okay. Here's the scoop."

He leaned against the wall, his eyes focused on her face. His expression lost all mirth as she relayed what

Shannon and Jayden had been through in the last twenty-four hours.

He pushed off and laid his hands on her shoulders. "Do me a favor. Text her back and get that Bob Morgan's number. I want to talk with him. I know one of the homicide detectives in Tallahassee. He may be able to help out."

"Seriously? How? Another frat brother like Grady?"

"No. We met at a seminar on new DNA detection methods last spring."

Ah, yes. She recalled when he went. And how out of sorts she'd felt that week knowing he wasn't around. "The one in Atlanta."

"Right. Tad Burns. We roomed together. He invited me to come visit him when I got some time off. I told him the same. Hasn't happened, though." He shrugged.

She texted Shannon as she shook her head. "The fact you met him months ago and were even roommates, and now he may be of help to us? Wow. God works in mysterious ways."

Chase gave her a head bob. "Trust me. I rely on His help all the time."

"I know." She gazed into his deep, blue eyes. "I'm glad you do."

He furrowed his eyebrows. "I think it might be wise to conduct some background checks on the staff at that hospice center, though. Just in case. Mrs. P. shouldn't have overdosed. If someone who works there is making mistakes like that, no wonder people are dying at the rate they are."

"Would you be allowed to?"

"No, not without a warrant. But I know someone at DADS . . ."

"Who?" She stopped mid texting.

He grinned. "It stands for the Texas Department of Aging and Disability Services, the agency that monitors these places. Name is Greg Hartman. He might be persuaded to make a visit."

Bailey chuckled. "Is there anyone you *don't* know?"

He glanced at the ceiling as he scratched his chin. "The current president of the United States for one, and also several movie stars come to mind." Then he glanced at her and smirked.

"I definitely need coffee." Shaking her head, Bailey started down the corridor again toward the cafeteria, with him shuffling to catch up to her side.

Leaf Me Alone

Chapter Twenty-two

Jayden pulled into Jacksonville early that afternoon. His wife looked as if her appetite had returned, so they stopped off to grab some food and ate it in the cab.

Shannon picked up her phone. "Maybe I should call Beverley and Parker Andersen to see if they are home."

He set his drink down. "You don't know if his wife knows about the cash donations he'd made to his dad, or if she even knew that he'd made contact with him, so you better not mention that."

"True. I'll say I wanted to tell them about his great aunt." She put the conversation on speakerphone when Beverley answered. She wet her lips before speaking, a sure sign her nerves were on edge. He patted her a shoulder to give her encouragement.

Her soft brown eyes met his, melting his heart all over again. Every. Time.

She squeezed his fingers and spoke into the receiver. "This is Shannon Johnson. The one you spoke with about Parker's dad, Manny. Parker never returned my call, so . . ."

"Yes. I recall who you are. I'm not sure how I can help you."

"Well, my husband is a long-hauler . . ."

"A what?"

"He drives an eighteen-wheeler and has a few days off after dropping off a shipment in Orlando. I was out here in Tallahassee anyway trying to locate Manny."

"Did you have any luck?"

"Not really. But I've never seen the Atlantic Ocean, so we decided to drive in your direction. I thought, maybe, I could drop by and tell Parker about his great aunt. I mean, if that is convenient and if he'd like that."

"Our daughter has a softball game at three but let me check."

As she waited Shannon glanced at Jayden. "I didn't exactly lie."

He chuckled at her contriteness. He'd married a good woman. "No, girl, you told her the truth. Just not the whole truth. And I get it. No sense putting a wedge between them if she doesn't know about his escapades to Tallahassee."

"If he made them. We still don't know how those envelopes of money got there."

He waggled his head as he tapped the steering wheel. "True. But if anyone can weave the conversation around to ask him that, I know you can."

Her eyes dropped. "Thanks, hon."

Beverley's voice came through the speakers again. Shannon's mouth formed an "O" and she raised the phone back to her lips. "Yes, we're still here."

"How about we meet at a restaurant I know south of downtown. It's famous for its pies. Say, two o'clock? I can text you the address."

Shannon's face searched his for confirmation.

Jayden shrugged. "Fine with me. You know I love pie." It wasn't as if they had a tight schedule. Still, he liked that she asked him.

"My husband says that sounds great. We look forward to meeting you. How will we recognize you?"

Beverley snickered. "Easy. We'll be the ones with the T-shirts that say West Duval Youth Association on them."

Shannon's lips moved after she hung up and Jayden knew she tried to memorize the name. He winked at her. "I got it. Remember, I grew up off Duval Street in Austin. Small world."

Her eyes glowed as they widened. "That's right! Gotta be a sign."

At a quarter until two, they pulled across the street from the pastel-painted, art deco café and parked the rig's cab. The air hung with humidity, and seagulls cawed above them. "How far are we from the beach?"

Jayden pulled up his GPS. "About a half-hour to the east. That's the St. John River we saw coming down King Street."

"That's a river? It is huge! I thought it was a bay or something."

He nodded and laced his arm through her elbow. "After we meet with the Andersens, how about we drive to the beach. Then you can stick those pretty little toes of yours in the ocean."

She danced on them. "Really? Can we?"

He protruded his lower lip. "Don't see why not. It's under two hours to Orlando and the coast isn't that much further away. Less than an hour's drive. We'd have time to splash around, find a seafood place for dinner, and still get there by dark or so. The car rental places stay open late on weekends I imagine."

"I'll call one and let them know we're coming. Then we can drive back to the hotel and get there by bedtime tonight." She stretched on to her tiptoes and planted a long kiss on his cheek. Yeah, her coming to Florida was a great idea, in spite of the fact it dwindled their ready cash supply.

He held her free hand as they crossed the street, suddenly feeling like a teenager again. He had two things he had to do, and soon. Help her find Manny Andersen and then find a job near San Antonio so he could be home with her more often.

They waited outside by the wrought iron fence that surrounded the restaurant. Within a few minutes, a middle-aged couple with the softball T-shirts walked up the sidewalk. Jayden waved.

The Andersens were a tad more gracious in their reception, which relieved Shannon. Maybe it was because they were meeting face to face in public and didn't want to create a scene. The two couples exchanged common pleasantries about the weather as strangers often do.

Since the atmosphere had thawed, Shannon relayed how much Mrs. Perkins had influenced her life as they all dug into wedges if key lime pie. "Here, I have a few pictures of her on my phone."

She called up her gallery of photos and swiped through them. Then she enlarged the one of Mrs. Perkins with her, Bailey, and Jessica and passed it across the table. "These are my best friends who also take her class."

Jayden recalled that day now. Bailey had taken the picture at a church picnic. The fact that they were chatting with the older woman that day hadn't hit his radar. As he listened to his wife speak of her mentor, he wished he'd gotten to know her a bit better. A new sense of urgency to find her nephew came over him. In fact, he owned it. He no longer was in this to appease his wife. This had become his mission, too. He entered the conversation.

"Parker, I know your parents divorced. But, do you recall anything about your dad that might help us locate him? We know Mrs. Perkins left you money in a saving account when you were growing up. It's a kind gesture to be able to help family out without ever expecting to be repaid." Jayden peered into his eyes, conveying a silent message that he and Shannon also knew about the money Parker had left for Manny.

Beverley turned to her husband. "I didn't know that."

He patted her arm. "Yeah, she did. Not much, but it was what she could do, I guess. Anyway, by the time I graduated from high school it was enough to get a used car. It seems my mom had contacted her when I was born, even though my dad and his aunt had parted ways. We never told Dad about the money. Well, I rarely ever saw him after we moved here anyway."

Jayden saw the door of opportunity creak open. "Did you ever reconnect with him?"

Parker's eyes narrowed just for a second. He wiped his mouth and set his fork down. "I tried a few times over the years. There were also times he tried to contact me. Mostly because he was down and out again and needed money."

Shannon shot Jayden a glance. He tried to convey to her with his eyes to wait a minute before she said anything. For once, she obeyed.

Beverley sat back in the booth. "We never would give him any though. He'd only waste it on booze and who knows what. I guess you both realize he was a derelict. Never paid child support, did he, honey?"

"I don't think he did." Parker cleared his throat and shifted in his seat.

Jayden decided to loosen the conversation ropes a tad. In his youth, he'd dabbled in rodeo and learned that broncs often bucked less if you eased up a bit on the reins. "Well, both my wife and I were surprised how green and lush Tallahassee is. Ever been there?"

Parker's mouth opened, but before he could answer, his wife did. "Oh my, yes. He goes all the time on business, don't you, dear? At least once a month. The corporate offices are located there, and they have meetings and such. But he's usually only gone a day or so."

So that's how the money got there. Jayden gave Parker a nod hopefully to let him know they knew about the envelopes of cash.

Parker glanced outside the picture window. "I knew Dad used to hang around the city, but I never saw him on the streets. Not that I'd recognize him. Still, I'd be lying if I said I never did a double-take whenever I saw an older homeless man downtown near headquarters."

"So, you wouldn't recognize him today if you saw him. We'd hoped maybe you could give us an idea of who we are looking for. It'd be easier."

Beverley tapped the table with her finger. "I think we have an old photo of him in his naval uniform amongst Parker's baby pictures. Martha gave us an album chronicling Parker's youth when we got married. I can take a snapshot of it and text it to you."

"Thanks, Beverley. That might help." Shannon smiled sweetly. Man, his wife could be a charmer.

Beverley dropped her eyes. "Not a problem. Happy to."

Then she shifted her attention to Parker. "Do you recall any distinguishing or unique features he might have had. Like a scar or a mole?"

Parker pressed his lips together. "Yeah. Now that you mention it. He had a bad pox mark above his left eyebrow, here." He pointed toward his own temple. "He was rather self-conscious of it, I think. It's funny what you remember." He scooted forward. "I have an image of me sitting on his lap and touching it. He slapped my hand away, yelled at me, and threw me to the floor. I landed right on my bottom. As I wailed, I think more from shock than pain, he and my mother really got into one of their screaming matches. I dashed to my room, shut the door, and buried my head in my pillow." He sighed. "I must have been about three or so."

Beverley pouted and grasped his hand. "Parker didn't

have a very happy childhood. Until his mother finally got the gumption to leave that slime. Thank goodness she did."

Parker remained silent but his Adam's apple wobbled. Jayden decided to let him loose from any more interrogation into his past. He half-rose from the booth and extended his hand. "Thanks. Sorry to dredge up bad memories. Listen. If you like, we can take a picture now and then forward it to one of Shannon's church friends, to show it to Mrs. Perkins. I think she'd really like that."

Shannon bounced in her seat. "Jayden. That is a great idea. I know it would make her final days a bit happier to see how well you turned out."

Beverley nodded. But Parker didn't take Jayden's hand. Instead, he eased his back into the booth. "I have a better idea." He turned to his wife. "Bev. I have to be in Tallahassee on Monday anyway. Why don't I follow them back this evening, and then after the meeting on Monday I can drive Mr. and Mrs. Johnson back to San Antonio. I'd like to see my great aunt before she . . ." He stopped and took a swallow of his sweet tea then set it back down. "If that is alright with you, Jayden."

Shannon glanced back and forth between them.

Jayden thought. The idea of another man driving them across the country didn't sit well with him. But the man seemed decent enough, even if he had been keeping secrets from his wife. "Okay. If Shannon agrees."

She laughed. "You mean we wouldn't have to take a long, stinky bus ride back to Texas? What do you think?"

All four of them chuckled. Then Jayden realized that after he handed over the rig in Orlando, he needed to rent a car to get back to Jasonville anyway. "Tell you what, man. I need to get this rig back to Orlando and my wife wants to stick her pinkies in the Atlantic Ocean. We'll rent a car, pick you up tonight about nine, and head to Tallahassee. We can split the cost if you like and take it to S.A. Then you can drive it back and save the wear and tear on your own car."

Parker grinned. "Sounds good. Thanks. What's your cell phone number? I'll text you mine."

Jayden gave it to him. The man keyed it in. In a second, his phone pinged. Jayden pulled it out of his pocket. "Got it."

Parker nodded and scooted back his chair. "See you at nine."

Jayden reached out his hand. "We are staying at the Starlight Motel in case you want to get a room."

"Right, I'll do that." Parker shook it in a manly grip.

The two couples said their goodbyes.

As Shannon and Jayden walked to the rig, she stopped. "Jayden?"

"What?"

"I'm thinking Parker knows where to find Manny. Did

you get that impression?"

He studied her face. "That's what I'm hoping. Once we get out of earshot of his wife, maybe he'll open up. And we can tell him about this Ernie character. It'll be an interesting ride back tonight. But for now, let's head for the beach and Orlando."

"Okay, time to come clean, man. Your wife isn't around now. We know about the hundred-dollar drop-offs." Jayden peered in the rearview mirror of the rental at their backseat passenger. A passing car's headlights flashed on his blank face.

Parker leaned forward. "Excuse me? What drop-offs?"

"Don't jive us, man. Bob Martin told us that he and Manny went to the post box on the fifteenth of every month to retrieve the envelopes of cash you secretly left for him."

"Who is Bob Martin? I don't know what you are talking about."

Jayden studied his face. The man either really played poker well or told the truth. "You've never been in contact with your father in Tallahassee?"

"Yes. I have. A few times. When the hospital would call me. Dad always listed me as his next of kin after Mom told the hospital to quit calling her parents each time he cratered. But the last time was a good five or six years ago. Dad swore he was staying clean this time." He sat back and shrugged. "Then again, he always said it."

Shannon shot a glance at Jayden. "It seems the last time he did tell you the truth. After he left the hospital, he entered a halfway house run by Bob Martin and went through his program. Even became an employee. But he left about a year ago when he got a real job."

"Doing what?"

"Janitorial work from what we gather."

Parker laughed, but it sounded melancholy. "Dad always loved to clean house. I recall him humming as he swept and mopped. My friends thought it was weird."

"Seems he landed a great job on the custodial staff of the state museum a few months back." Shannon craned her neck to smile at their passenger.

Jayden swallowed. "Seemed" was right. Considering it was probably Ernie impersonating him. He caught Shannon's glance as they telepathed the same message to each other.

"Really?" Parker's voice lifted. "And this Bob fellow told you I sent my dad money each month?"

Jayden nodded into the mirror. "That's right. He had a ledger. And there's more. But you may not like to hear it." Jayden told him what Ernie had told them about taking his dad's identity. He left out the part that he and Shannon, and perhaps Bob, thought Ernie had murdered his dad. That tidbit could wait.

"Ernie told us he took your father's name years ago and pretended to be him, but Bob Martin swears the man who he knows as Manny had a pox mark just like your dad. Ernie doesn't, only a small scar. That's what's puzzling us. Exactly when did Ernie assume his identity, and if not years ago, why tell us that? We were hoping you could shed some light on this mystery."

Parker ran his hand down his face, which had turned considerably paler. After several minutes he spoke. "Look, my mind needs to take this in. I had no idea any of this stuff went on. But I swear by all that is holy, I never met this Bob, or anyone named Ernie, and I never put money in a post office box for my dad."

Shannon's mouth dropped open.

Jayden glanced at her and then back to Parker. "Then who did?"

Leaf Me Alone

Chapter Twenty-three

Bailey's phone rang, and she recognized the number as Chase's private cell. Why would he be calling in the middle of the day on a Saturday? They didn't have plans to see each other.

"Hey, Chase. How's it going?"

There was a hesitation on the other end of the line, then she heard him clear his throat. "Okay, I called Greg Hartman."

"Excuse me?"

"The guy from DADS. I told him it might sound strange to complain that people in a hospice center were dying too soon, but I trusted your instincts. They'd always been pretty accurate in the past."

Warmth spread over her chest and she clutched her heart. To hear him say that meant more to her than she'd expected it would. She blinked. "And?"

"And, he said in his ten years with DADS, he'd often had people call to complain about an agency. Their loved ones' diapers were always soiled. The place stank. The food was wretched. A nurse seemed uncaring. But never anything like that."

"Oh. I see." Her mood sunk like a pebble dropped into a glass of water.

"No, it's good." Chase's voice quickened. "The fact that this was a new type of complaint got his attention. He said there was no reason to not check it out because he knew I wouldn't have called him if I didn't believe there was some legitimate concern."

"Really? That's great. Thanks, Chase."

"There's more. Twenty minutes later he called me back. He said when he spoke to the receptionist she sounded very pleasant, almost too pleasant. He asked to speak to the director and after being placed on hold for several minutes, a woman named Roberta Louise Stoller answered."

"I see. And what did she have to say?" Bailey scooted forward in her chair.

"Greg didn't give her time to respond. He told her he was Greg Hartman of the Department on Aging and Disabilities Services and that his office had a phone call from a reputable source asking him to investigate the recent deaths at her facility. He told her he'd be there tomorrow morning at nine-thirty and for her to have the records of the last ten deceased patients available for his review."

"Wow."

"Yeah, then he chuckled. He told me he asked for her direct email so he could send the formal request on letterhead with all the necessary forms and identifying information. Unless of course, she'd prefer it to go to the general office's inbox. She stuttered and spouted her personal email off to him then hung up abruptly."

"Do you think she'll comply? I mean will she have time to doctor the paperwork?"

"Bailey, let's not go there at this point. Let's let Greg do his thing. He knows the ins and outs better than you or I. If there is anything fishy, he'll snag it."

She raised her eyes to the ceiling and shot up a quick prayer. "I hope so, Chase. I don't know which to pray for, that I'm mistaken or that I'm correct."

His voice softened. "Pray for the truth to be revealed and for God to take care of all concerned. Gotta run. I'll see you in church, okay? Save me a seat."

He hung up. Bailey sat there with her phone to her chin. His godly wisdom pierced that thick wall a tad more and several more bricks tumbled. Perhaps he truly was the man she needed in her life, for the rest of her life. Could it be God's will? She couldn't help but grin as she whispered to the ceiling. "I have to admit, a large part of me hopes so."

With Mrs. Perkins more stable, Bailey felt a bit more comfortable about leaving her alone for a few hours while she went to church and then dashed back to the hospice center to gather the lady's belongings. Even if they discharged her in a few days, no way was Mrs. P. going back there! Not if Bailey had any say in the matter.

Chase, of course, had to work after church services, even though it was Sunday. Crime didn't take the day off. But he reassured her that Greg had texted him to say he was already at the facility. If anything developed, he would let Chase know, and he'd pass it along to Bailey. Then Chase squeezed her fingers and walked to his car.

She pulled her subcompact car into one of the visitor slots and climbed out. She opened the trunk to retrieve three empty boxes she'd fished out of the apartment dumpster, courtesy of the person down the hall who had just moved in. They'd even left a half-used roll of tape and some wrapping paper in one of the boxes. A serendipity for sure. She shook her head at the realization God truly was in the details . . . not the devil, like the old adage said.

She shifted the bulky folds of cardboard under her arm

and headed up the walkway. The receptionist motioned to her.

"I'm here to collect Mrs. Grace Perkins' belongings. She is still in the hospital and will be for a few days. I am not sure they will return her here or not, so I told her I'd come get her a few changes of clothes and pack up her room, just in case you all need it."

"Wait here, please." The receptionist unwound herself from her secretary chair and went down the hallway to the administration offices. In a few minutes, a business-suited woman prissed down the hallway, her high heels echoing off the linoleum tiled floor. Bailey read her tag as she approached— Roberta Louise Stoller. The director was here on a Sunday? Hm. Gathering medical records perhaps? She stifled a smirk.

The director flashed Bailey a stern expression with a slight jut of her chin. "I'm sorry. We can't allow you to disturb Mrs. Perkins's things without her explicit permission. If you can have her sign these forms, then we can proceed." She handed them to Bailey with a snap of her wrist.

"Fine. I'll be back in an hour, then." Bailey snatched the paper and headed for the front exit. Then she halted. No need to be rude no matter how irked she felt. They had protocols to follow. She pivoted on her heel and plastered on her sweetest smile. "I am sure it will relieve Mrs.

Perkins' mind to know you are so thorough and conscientious about your residents."

Mrs. Stoller's expression softened, if only for a split-second. She nodded and clicked her heels back down the corridor.

Bailey put on some praise music to calm her nerves as she drove back to the hospital. The last twenty-four hours had been taxing, but now Mrs. P. lay safe and sound and well-guarded by the hospital staff. When she arrived at Room 432, she found her mentor softly snoring. Bailey's shoulders slackened but her brow furrowed. The woman in the bed didn't resemble her vibrant Bible study leader at all. When did she become so frail and her complexion so pallor?

She slid into the visitor chair and propped her feet against the windowsill. Pulling up her Bible app on her tablet, she began to read the chapter in John they were to discuss next week. When the rays filtered through the blinds to hit the illuminated screen, she smiled. It was as if God patted her on the shoulder—or read over it.

The strands of light must have reached the old woman's face because she stirred and scrunched her eyelids. Bailey set the device down and twisted the rod to further close the slats.

"No, it's fine. I like the sunshine." Mrs. Perkins' voice sounded weak but clear.

Bailey walked closer to her bedside. "Hi, I didn't want to disturb your nap. I have a form for you to sign giving me permission to go pack your things and bring them to you. Protocol."

With a sigh, she nodded and held out a shaky hand for the forms and pen. "All this rigmarole for a few pairs of underwear and a nightie."

Bailey smiled. "Well, I am going to pack up your other things, too, in case they need to use the room. If the doctors decide you should return, we can carry it back."

"I'm not going back." Her voice shook a bit.

"I understand. We'll see what we can do."

Her arthritic fingers snatched Bailey's arm. "Please, don't let me return there. They tried to kill me. I'm sure of it."

Fear flashed in her baby blue eyes. An emotion Bailey had never witnessed from her. It unnerved her. She gulped and patted the woman's hands. "Of course not. I'll speak to the service coordinator. In the meantime, I heard from Shannon, and they are making progress in Florida. So, you rest tight and get stronger, okay?"

A warm glow began to ooze over her face. "That is good news. I so want to see him."

Bailey felt the love, exhibited in her face, travel down the woman's arm, through her fingers to Bailey's and up into her own heart. She swallowed. "I'll be back soon with your things."

On the drive back to the hospice facility, Bailey's resolve strengthened. She pulled over to get a bottled water from a convenience store and phoned Chase to let him know what Mrs. Perkins had said and about the fearful expression on her face.

"Okay. I'll let Greg know. He may want to come interview her."

"Thanks, Chase. I really mean that."

"Anytime, angel. Sure you don't want me to come help?"

"No, I'm fine. She doesn't have that much. A few pieces of clothing along with some photos and figurines. She probably wouldn't want you to see her unmentionables anyway."

He laughed and it made her chuckle as well. "True. Okay, then. I'll call you later."

"Take care, Chase. Stay safe."

"Always."

She clicked off and once again entered with the cardboard boxes tucked under one arm. She slipped the form onto the counter and gave the receptionist the sweet professional smile she often used at work to calm down nervous taxpayers as she poured over their bank statements. "I think this is all in order."

The receptionist glanced it over and nodded. "Sign in

here and let me make a copy of your ID for the record."

Bailey set the boxes down and pulled out her driver's license. The receptionist made a copy, confirmed that the signatures matched, and stapled the form to it. "You're good to go. If you need help, let me know and I'll get one of the orderlies to carry her things to your car."

It took longer than she anticipated. Not that Mrs. P. had a lot of things, but each one deserved to be handled with delicate care. And she wanted to savor every item because they gave her a unique window into this wonderful woman's past. She resisted the urge to sit and thumb through the highlighted pages of the woman's well-worn and much-loved Bible and examine all of the notes. That might be an invasion of privacy, and besides, it would take hours and hours. Then a pang hit her heart. She'd have all the time in the world to do that after . . . she shook that thought away and gingerly wrapped the holy book inside the lady's robe.

Mrs. P. had brought a suitcase that Bailey used to pack her toiletries and clothes. The rest she sorted into two boxes, photos in one and memorabilia in the other. The orderly brought a cart, loaded the things onto it, and wheeled it to her car as the sun began to sneak behind the hills to the west. Bailey drove to her apartment to first feed her cat. She decided to leave the boxes in the trunk until Chase could help her put them in her storage closet.

After she pulled into her apartment complex, she bounded up the stairs, two at a time. Her footsteps stopped short at her door. A note was taped to it. She fumbled with her keys as she pulled the folded card off the wood and unlocked her door.

The note fell to the carpet inside her door as she balanced on one foot to kick the door shut. Whose visit had she missed? She set down her purse and picked up her cat with one hand and the card with the other. "Hungry, baby?" She snuggled Bower the Meower against her chin.

She struggled to unfold the card with one hand and caught a glimpse of the words inside.

Didn't your mother teach you not to snoop?

She gasped and set her cat down, then dug in her purse to find her phone. With a raspy breath, she spoke in the command. "Call Chase Montgomery, mobile."

She glanced back at the card. Had she read that correctly? But the words were there in black, block letters. And the sentence that followed them sent a chill across her shoulders.

Stop now or Mrs. Perkins may not be the only one in the hospital tomorrow.

Chapter Twenty-four

Shannon flicked on her phone as the three of them drove back to Tallahassee. "Oh. Bailey texted me a few hours ago. I didn't hear it ping."

She opened and read Bailey's message with a gasp. Then she pulled up the photocopy of the threatening note Bailey had added as an attachment. A small relief flowed over her when she saw Chase's fingers holding it in an evidence bag. She recognized his academy ring.

"Is she okay?" Jayden's eyebrows met across his forehead as he glanced at her before returning his attention to the road.

Shannon sighed. "Yeah. Chase is with her."

Jayden clucked his teeth. "I cannot believe she is getting threats. Again. I mean the woman is a magnet for them. How many did she get while digging into her family's past?"

"A few. I got one, too. Remember?"

"Yeah." Jayden grasped her hand. "It could have been you getting this one if you weren't here in Florida. Maybe you ladies are right. Perhaps there is someone at that hospice place who is responsible for these deaths. Let's hope Chase's friend uncovers something tangible."

"She's not going back there, is she?" Parker's tone in the back seat had a concerned pitch to it.

"No, Bailey says the service coordinator at the hospital is looking for other options. But Mrs. P. will be in the hospital a few more days anyway. That's where we'll head when we get to San Antonio." Shannon twisted her torso toward the back of the car. "She'll be fine. You'll get to meet her."

"Well, I'd like to find Dad as well. This money thing is eerie. Why would he say it was from me?"

Jayden shrugged his linebacker shoulders. "I tell you, man. It gets stranger the more I think about it. I can't wrap my brain around it. Perhaps he was a paid informant for the vice squad but made up the story to protect his identity?"

Shannon shot him a get-real-bud expression. "Now who is sounding like a whodunit TV movie?"

"Well, you have another theory?"

Her brain began to whirl. Could it be Manny Andersen pretended to be homeless and destitute in order to pass along info to the narcs all these years? No, his hospitalizations had to have been real. "I don't buy it. Bob Morgan is a savvy dude. He wouldn't have let him stay in the program, much less become an employee . . ."

Jayden lifted a hand off the steering wheel and pointed at her. "Unless he's in on it. Maybe he agreed to have a plant in his facility."

"A what?"

"I think your husband means someone sent there to blend in." Parker added his opinion to the conversation. "Maybe to make sure all the residents stayed clean."

Shannon nodded. "Oh, right. But surely he'd have told us."

"Unless the investigation is still ongoing." Jayden returned his grip to the steering wheel.

"There is still the issue about the pox mark. The man we saw definitely did not have one." Shannon crossed her arms over her chest. "Which means Ernie isn't Manny."

"Then where is my dad?"

"I wish we knew, Parker. I wish we knew." She shifted her gaze to the rearview mirror to see Parker slouch. Her heart tore at one corner for him. Poor guy. A lot to absorb all at once. Not to mention stirring up all the drama of the past.

"My father may be dead, right?" His voice sounded a bit shaky.

"Let's hope not, man. But yes, he might." Jayden

swallowed and kept his eyes on the road.

Shannon scanned Bailey's text again. What had they stumbled into? A possible murder, fraud, and identity theft? Or a cover-up for a sting operation. And back home her best friend faced threats while her mentor had almost been killed by an overdose.

She thought back to Jessica's being kidnapped and threatened while she sought to discover enough information to exonerate her birth father. Bailey and Shannon had both received threats while investigating Bailey's grandparents' accident back in the day.

Who knew finding relatives could be so dangerous?

Her head ached.

Chapter Twenty-five

By the time they pulled into the motel parking lot, Shannon's eyes were heavy and her brain mushy. Parker had made a reservation as they drove from Jacksonville. They dropped him off at his room, four doors down from theirs.

Shannon plopped onto her back on the bed. "Man, what a day."

Jayden set his keys down and sat next to her. "You do keep things interesting, girl."

She propped herself on her elbows. "I can't get a handle on this. Who would have kept dropping off money? Can we trust Parker is telling us the truth?"

"I think so. He seems to be a decent guy, and his eyes really got wide when we mentioned it. Now tell me again what's this all about with Bailey?"

Shannon read him the text once more, and then the

longer email she had sent an hour later once Chase had left. "See? Now Chase agrees there may be something weird going on. He has a friend of his with that state agency investigating and then within hours Bailey gets threats? I'm worried."

"Maybe we should head back to Alamo City with Parker and forget trying to locate Manny."

She sat up and curled her legs under her as she faced him. "But that would be breaking a promise, Jay."

He placed both hands on her knees, his eyes searching hers. "Mrs. P. had no idea things would get so complicated. It might be best to let Bob and the local police handle this. They can find this Ernie dude and find out what really happened."

She slumped her forehead against his chest. "I guess."

He lifted her chin with his thumb. She blinked back the weariness in her eyes. Concern spread over his face, and then a tender expression he only gave to her. It made her heart warm.

"Look at it this way, girl. She wanted to see her long-lost relative before she passed on. We are bringing her Manny's son. The one she never met but cared enough for to put money into a savings account all those years. She'll be ecstatic."

Shannon threw her arms around his neck. "You're right. Thanks, hon."

He kissed her, yanked off her sandals, pulled back the covers, and folded her into them. "Get some sleep." Her eyes closed as she watched him head to the bathroom, pulling his shirt over his head.

Her phone rang the next morning. Shannon patted the bedside table until she felt the coolness of the glass, swiped the screen, and squinted to see who had the audacity to call her this early. Then she saw Bob's name and the time. 9:32 a.m. Wow, she hadn't slept that long into the morning in years.

She cleared her throat. "Hey, Bob. What's up?"

Jayden rustled next to her and rubbed his eyes.

"I have news. A detective lifted some fingerprints from a poem I had that Manny wrote while he lived here."

She stifled a yawn. "They can do that?"

"Yep. And he sent them to a friend he knew in the NCIS."

"Naval crimes unit, like on TV?" She sat up. Jayden did as well, his face forming a giant question mark expression. She punched the speaker button and set the phone down between them. "Go on. I've got you on speaker so Jayden can hear, too."

"Hey, Jayden. As I said, we got some good prints and Detective Burns sent them to a naval friend. They found a match. The navy still had his fingerprints on file from when the police requested them back in 1988. They kept them since they were evidence in a crime. Go figure, right?"

Shannon shook the rest of the sleep from her head. "Yeah. Has to be a God-thing. So . . ."

"So, the man who was in residence here was definitely Manny Andersen. Do you still have the note Ernie gave you from Parker?"

She glanced at Jayden. "Yes. I do. In my suitcase."

"Bring it, and Parker, to the Tallahassee police headquarters downtown. I'll meet you there. Or do you want me to come get you?"

"That would be great since you know your way around. We'll let Parker know. Say in an hour?"

She hung up as Jayden grabbed for the motel phone. "I'll ring his room while you shower."

She pecked his cheek, then grabbed a fresh set of clothes and dashed into the small cubicle the motel deemed as the bathroom. Taking the fastest shower since she was in summer camp, she reentered the room to find her husband already dressed. "Parker already ate breakfast. They shut down the buffet at ten, so I'll go grab us a bagel and cream cheese. Want some juice?"

"If they have it."

"You make coffee. I'll be right back. Then we will head for the police station."

"Okay. Thanks, hon."

He nodded and slipped out the door. When he

returned, she had put on a pair of slacks and blouse and the pot had gurgled its final grunt and hiss to let them know the brewing cycle had finished. She poured him a cup as he placed their breakfast on the small bistro table by the window.

They ate in a hurried silence. A tap sounded. Jayden wiped his mouth, stood, and peered through the peephole. Then mouthed the word *Parker* to Shannon as he jerked open the door. "Come in, man. We'll fill you in."

"So, you want to see if the fingerprints on the note that I supposedly wrote are my father's or this dude who is impersonating him?"

"You are sure you didn't write it, man?"

"How could I? I didn't know about this monthly drop until you told me last night in the car."

Shannon showed it to Parker but wouldn't let him touch it. She still questioned if he told them the truth. The police would want both Parker's and her fingerprints for elimination. If the document didn't contain any of his, then they'd know someone else penned it.

They waited outside for Bob. He drove up in the Better Life Ahead van. "Hop in."

Jayden introduced the two men to each other, and then he and Parker slid into the back seat, leaving the front passenger seat for Shannon. She thanked him. Considering how fast she'd shoveled down that bagel, it already sat in her stomach like a big doughy lump. Riding in the back seat might dislodge it into her throat.

Within fifteen minutes, they had reached the station. Bob lead the way inside. He showed the policeman at the information desk Detective Burns' card. The officer motioned them to a row of chairs against the wall and punched in some numbers on the phone. Shannon watched as the other people in the station buzzed about like bees in a field of foxglove. None of them smiled.

A tall, slender, middle-aged man in a brown suit jacket and no tie came to greet them. He acknowledged Bob and then extended his hand to each. "Tad Burns. This way, please."

He led them to an examination room. Shannon felt her hastily eaten breakfast flip, but when Jayden placed his hand on the small of her back, his warm strength calmed her down.

Tad must have picked up on her hesitancy. "Sorry. I know it is an interrogation room, but my office is too small for all of us."

She accepted his explanation and sat where he indicated.

"Mr. Andersen?" He motioned with his hand for Parker to sit next to her. Bob and Jayden stood against the wall.

He pushed a form across to them with a pen laying on

top. "We'd like to record the conversation, with your permission of course. Protocol. Just need each of you to sign, please."

Parker handed her the pen. "Ladies first."

She wrote her name on the permission slip and then slid it over to him. As he inscribed, she glanced at Tad Burns who smiled back at her with a slight nod. Yes, fresh prints captured. Parker pushed the paper and pen back to Tad, who gently shoved it to the side. "Thanks. Okay. Let's begin."

He briefly relayed what had transpired and how they had lifted the fingerprints from the poem. "My buddy at NCIS was able to locate some documents that still revealed Manny Andersen's fingerprints on them. And Bob, here, recalled a poem Manny once wrote that he'd had framed and hung in his office."

Shannon bobbed her head. "I've read that you get reliable prints from a piece of paper."

"Evidently, paper is a great conduit. It absorbs the oils in our fingers. Bob, I'm glad you were smart enough not to try and take the paper out of the frame yourself, possibly contaminating the evidence."

"Glad I was able to help." Bob tucked his hands into his pockets.

Shannon glanced at Jayden then Parker. "And?"

"They were clear enough to lift from the paper. I had

it run through the AFIS, which is an automated system, and confirmed a match from the DD214 that Manny gave you, Bob, upon entering the program. I contacted a buddy of mine at NCIS, as I said. They were able to locate his records of discharge and pull prints from that. I got the results back a few hours ago. All three matched. The same person who was discharged as Manny Andersen gave Bob his documentation and also wrote the poem during his stay."

A chill raced up Shannon's spine.

Tad eyed her and then Jayden. "You say this Ernie fellow told you he had assumed Manny Andersen's identity before that date?"

"That's right." Shannon glanced at her husband who gave her a wink for encouragement. "He told us at least six years ago."

"Describe him."

Shannon did, including the lack of the pox mark Bob Morgan and Parker verified Manny Andersen had on his temple. "He did have a small scar, which appeared almost healed, here." She swiped her finger at the outer tip of her eyebrow.

"And you have the note he handed you?"

She pulled it from her purse.

Parker bent to scan it once more. "That's not from me. I swear it. The handwriting doesn't even resemble mine."

Tad shoved a new piece of paper across the table. "Mind writing it out for me? I'll dictate."

Parker didn't hesitate. He scrawled the words without a hint of apprehension. Then he pushed it back to the detective. He took a minute comparing the two. "I'm no handwriting analyst, but they look different enough to me. I'll send it to the lab to verify. And see if they can lift prints from the original note. Then we'll see what turns up."

Jayden pushed off from the wall and spoke for the first time. "What are we looking at? Fraud? Identity theft?"

Tad sat back and laced his fingers behind his head. "From what Bob has told me, yes. I have a BOLO out for this Ernie character. Mrs. Johnson, I'd like you to get with one of our sketch artists. They have a computer program which can quickly make a rendition of the man you met. That would help us immensely."

"Sure. Happy to. Will you be needing anything else from us?"

"Not at this point, other than permission to get your fingerprints. Yours as well, Mr. Andersen." He glanced at Jayden. "Did you touch the note?"

He shrugged. "I can't recall, honestly. Do you, hon?"

Shannon shook her head.

"Better get mine as well." He rubbed his chin.

Shannon could tell being in the police station unnerved her hubby a bit. Once, in his early twenties, he had been caught in a DUI. He'd spent thirty-six hours in the drunk tank and the experience had made him a teetotaler. The memory of it still sent a small shiver through his mind, though. She could see it by how hard he swallowed.

She rose and slipped her hand into his. "Thanks, hon."

He stood a bit taller. "No problem. I want them to nail this guy. He's the only one who knows where Manny is."

An hour later, the four were ready to leave the police station. Tad met them in the hallway. "Did you leave a number where you can be reached with the desk clerk?"

Jayden sucked in his breath. "Yes. We'd plan to head back to Texas today. Parker wants to meet his great aunt before she passes, and she isn't long for this world. We can leave, right?"

When Shannon heard the words "before she passes" from Jayden's lips, it hitched her nerves. Like scratching a scab, it made her heart bleed a bit again.

"Can you stick around another twenty-four hours?"

Jayden turned to Shannon and Parker. "That'll mean paying for two hotel rooms for another day."

Parker reached for his wallet. "I'll pay for them. It's the least I can do. And I'll swing for the gas back to Texas as well."

Jayden swung around to face him. "You sure?'

He swatted the comment away. "Yeah. You've already paid for the rental car. Drop me back at the motel. I can get some work done while you two go play tourist. Tallahassee is a cool city."

Jayden turned to the detective. "I gather he didn't show up for work at the museum last night, right?"

Tad rolled his eyes. "How'd ya guess?"

Everyone chuckled, which broke some of the tension. Tad shook their hands and walked with them to the front entrance. Shannon stopped mid-stride. "Is there anything we can do? Research, background work? Chase may have told you my friends and I helped solve two crimes recently. If we can help in any way . . ."

"Yeah. He sort of mentioned it." Tad grinned and opened the door for them. "Thanks, but we've got this."

Shannon felt her cheeks warm.

Parker's face puckered in puzzlement.

Jayden leaned to his ear. "I'll explain it to you later on the way to Texas."

As they walked to the curb, Tad answered her question more thoroughly. "We got his employment records from the museum and have located his apartment. Of course, it had been cleared out. The guy is in the wind. But the photocopy of the driver's license the manager had on file has been verified to be that of a Manuel Parker Andersen. And the signatures on the lease matched those on his license. And, those on the paperwork he'd signed at Better Life Ahead when he first came four years ago."

"Ernie could have had plenty of time to practice it." Jayden leaned against a parking meter and crossed his arms.

"True. I can tell you this. The manager was more than happy to let us search the place without a warrant. Though Manny had left it spotless, we'd hoped to find some forensic evidence." He let out a breath.

"And?" Shannon shifted her weight to the other foot.

"We did lift a few fingerprints on the inside of the fridge, but no evidence of blood was found. No sign of a struggle like new scuff marks on the floor or walls."

Parker let out a shaky breath. "That's good, right?"

Tad gave him a slight shrug.

Parker's face fell. Shannon's heart went out to him. Though he had lost contact, Manny Andersen was his father. She realized how much this must upset him. It urged her even more to do something other than sightsee. "Maybe he had a friend at work we could go speak with, or at his old job. Where did you say that was, Bob?"

"He worked at a plastic surgery clinic. Runner, janitor, odd jobs. I called in a favor to get him hired. I'd helped a relative of one of the doctors get his life started again."

Tad shifted his weight. "Hold on. What's the clinic's name?"

Bob cocked his head. "Tallahassee Face and Body Renewal. Why?"

Tad turned to Jayden and Shannon. "You two stated that Ernie didn't sport the huge pox mark that Manny had on his face, correct?"

They glanced at each other. Shannon responded for both of them. "Yes. So?"

"But this guy, who claims to have had permission to assume his identity, had a small scar in the same general region?"

Shannon nodded.

"What if he had the mark removed?"

Bob shook his head. "It was huge. He got it from when he had chickenpox as a child. He said all his life kids at school and then his mates in the Navy kidded him about it. They called him Moonie instead of Manny because he had a crater."

Tad's eyes narrowed. "Even so. It might be worth investigating. Plastic surgeons can do amazing things."

"How could he afford such a thing?" Parker scoffed.

Tad lifted his shoulders in a slight shrug. "Maybe he overheard something and used it to his advantage. Or perhaps, as with you, Bob, he won them over. The man seems to have a knack for getting people to like and trust him."

"Then you are saying Ernie could really be my father and made up the whole story in order to remain anonymous?" Parker's voice cracked.

"It's possible."

Bob took a step forward. "You have to understand, these homeless folks are wary of attracting attention. Distrust is deeply seated in them. They learn to fade into the woodwork when they want to. It could be that Manny simply does not want to have any association with his past, though I honestly thought he was well past that fear. I still find it hard to believe that he'd come up with this ruse." He shook his head and glanced at the street.

Tad narrowed his eyes. "Let's see what the lab says when they compare the fingerprints on the note with the ones we found in his apartment this morning and the ones on the poem."

Chapter Twenty-six

Parker sat in the back seat with his lips pressed together all the way back to the motel. Bob dropped them off and agreed to let them know if he heard anything from Tad Burns. They agreed to do the same.

Shannon turned to Parker. "What can we do for you?"

The man blinked, and she noticed his eyelids had reddened. "I need to be alone for a while. You two go get lunch or something. If you hear anything from the detective, let me know. I'll be in my room."

He shoved his hands in his pockets and shuffled away.

"Wow, this has hit him hard." Jayden sighed as he swiped the fob to open their door.

"Wouldn't you be a bit overwhelmed right now?" Shannon entered the motel room. "I hope he remembers to pay for tonight. Check out time is in twenty minutes."

Jayden sat on the bed and grabbed the phone receiver.

"I'll call. They have our credit card on file."

When he did, he learned they had just hung up with Parker. He cupped his hand over the receiver. "They're paid for."

She smiled. In spite of all that must be racing through his mind, Parker Andersen had remembered his promise. Her esteem for the man soared. Martha Andersen Walters had done a fine job raising him. She looked forward to seeing Mrs. P.'s face when they met.

Which reminded her. She hadn't heard from Bailey. She pulled her phone from her purse and began clicking her thumbs.

Jayden grabbed two of the pillows, fluffed them, and leaned his scalp against the headboard. "Texting Bailey?"

"Uh, huh. Do you mind?"

He closed his eyes. "Nope. You two chat. I'm resting my brain a while."

Within a few minutes, his soft snores could be heard. Shannon smirked. The man had to be tired. He'd driven all over the state. But then again, he was used to doing that . . . until now.

The idea of him now being unemployed punched her in the gut. What were they going to do? She ran a profitable business, but no way would it make up for his income, too. She shuffled it aside to a corner of her brain she'd learn to label "For God to Handle." Instead, she briefly filled

Bailey in on their adventure at the police station. Her friend didn't need to know about Jayden's situation just yet.

Bailey responded. *Wow. This is getting weird. I'm sorry I ever got us all involved in genealogy and long-lost relative seeking. Can I tell Chase?*

Shannon chuckled as she typed that Tad Burns had probably already been in contact with him.

What can I do?

Exactly what Shannon had asked and got no response. *Keep Mrs. P. happy. Don't tell her about Parker, okay? Or about Manny being Ernie, if he is.*

In a second, Bailey's response pinged. *She doesn't know a thing. I keep telling her you and Jayden are trying to track him down and have some good leads.*

Is she getting better? Then Shannon caught herself and shook her head. *Well, you know what I mean.*

Yes, and yes. The social worker at the hospital is looking into other places for her to go when they discharge her, probably tomorrow.

Tomorrow? And they were stuck in Florida. It would take them another day to drive back to Texas, and that is if they drove straight through. She told Bailey to let her know and clicked off her phone.

Her husband lay with his mouth partially open, his eyes shut in dreamland. And her stomach suddenly felt empty.

She snatched the room fob and slipped down the corridor to the vending machines. She decided on an apple juice and a bag of peanuts. Then punched in D7 for some M&M's. Sometimes, a girl just needed chocolate.

As she carried the snacks back to the room, she heard a thud of footsteps following her.

Shannon turned to see a pale-faced Parker Andersen hurrying to catch up with her. He waved his cell phone.

"What is it?"

He stopped and placed his hands on his knees to catch his breath.

She waited.

"Tad Burns called. He says the fingerprints all match."

"Wait. You mean the ones on the note, in the apartment, and on the poem are all by the same person. He's sure?"

"Without a doubt, those were his words. And he obtained the records from the Navy. Identical. Manny Andersen definitely lived in that apartment up until a few days ago. No other prints except the super's were anywhere to be found."

Shannon set her peanuts, juice, and candy down on the carpeted hallway. She stared at the maroon, blue, and tan pattern only motels and office buildings would ever consider purchasing. What made her think of that again?

"I'm confused. Who is Ernie, then?"

Parker shuffled his feet. "That's the other thing. Burns went over to that plastic surgeon's office and confirmed that my father worked there up until seven months ago. And get this, he said they had developed a new procedure for minimizing pox marks and tags. He agreed to be one of their test subjects."

An icy chill rushed over her body. "What are you saying, Parker?"

"According to what the doctor told Burns, my father had the pox mark repaired. Between minor surgery, skin grafts, and ointments, all that is left is a small scar."

Shannon touched her outer eyebrow. "Here?"

He bounced his head up and down rapidly, his eyes wide with emotion. "That's what I understand."

She shook her head as if to tumble the information into some form of logical sense.

Parker swayed on his feet and rubbed his hands as she processed the information.

Shannon raised her gaze to meet his eyes. "So that means . . ."

"Yes. Ernie is my father. He made up the whole story."

"But what about the money drops? Bob went with him. He says they were there."

Parker puffed a breath from his cheeks. "I have no clue. I reiterated to Detective Burns that I never sent my father any money. I had no idea where he was or if he was even alive until today."

Shannon rubbed her temple. The cool droplets from her juice, still on her fingers, eased the tension developing into a headache. "Do you think your father and Bob made this all up?"

Parker crossed his arms. "I don't know. But I do know one thing. My father doesn't want to be found. And Burns says, given this new information, he sees no evidence of a crime." Suddenly his mood deflated like a balloon with a pin in it.

"What do you want to do?"

He puffed out a long breath. "Head to Texas. Even if my father doesn't want to see her, I do." He almost spat the word "father" as if it left a bad taste in his mouth. "I'll go pack."

Shannon's mind still felt jumbled. "But the hotel said you paid for the rooms. Why don't we wait until the morning?"

"I'd rather not." With his head bent, he turned to walk back to his room.

Shannon stood there, her brain not yet assimilating all of what he'd said. Something bugged her. She didn't know what, but she wanted to find out. She recalled visiting her grandmother when she was ten. They had spent all week putting together a jigsaw puzzle of a windmill in a field of tulips. Granny had gotten it at a garage sale. Except they couldn't finish it. Four or five pieces had evidently been mislaid by the previous owners. The pair hunted all over her grandmother's house for the missing parts. No luck.

Her grandmother had sighed and rocked the pouting Shannon on her lap. "It's okay, sugar. We got most of it done. And we accomplished a lot in a short while. Be proud of that."

Shannon had tried but couldn't quite get there. She couldn't now either. A few small pieces of this mystery didn't fit. She needed to find them. Trouble was, she didn't have a picture on a box top to let her know which ones were missing.

She picked up her food and went to wake her husband.

Jayden loaded the baggage in the back of the car. "But we said we'd stay another day."

Shannon placed her hand on his arm. "Evidently we don't need to now. And Parker really wants to leave. This has all gotten to him. It has to hurt that his father made up this story to fool us and then disappear again."

He rested his other hand on the lid of the open trunk. "Yeah. Probably dredges up a lot of childhood stuff for him. Poor guy. Here he comes."

Parker sauntered over with his duffel and slung it next to their things. "Ready to hit the road."

His smile didn't quite grow large enough to convince her. She swallowed and stepped away. "Let's head out, then."

Jayden shrugged and closed the trunk. "I'll drive first, then maybe when we hit Baton Rouge we can switch off."

"Fine with me, man." Parker opened the back door and slid into the passenger.

Shannon yanked on Jayden's shirt as he reached to open the door for her. She lowered her voice. "I am not comfortable leaving. Something isn't jibing."

He rested his arm on the top of the rental car. "And you bring this up now?"

She kicked the ground with her toe. "I've been mulling it over trying to ignore this feeling in the pit of my gut." She rubbed her waist.

"What doesn't sit right?"

She shielded her eyes from the afternoon sun bouncing off the cars in the parking lot. "Why make up the story about the money? It doesn't make sense."

"To add credence to why Manny would let Ernie assume his identity. Otherwise, why would he?"

"Then Bob lied to us as well? Why?"

From inside the car, they heard Parker's voice. "My thoughts as well. Maybe we should go ask him."

Shannon then realized the window had been lowered. She widened her eyes at Jayden who sighed. "Get in, girl."

Instead of heading to I-10, the three drove to The Better Life Ahead. Bob Morgan had some explaining to do.

Leaf Me Alone

Chapter Twenty-seven

Chase tapped on the hospital room door. Bailey felt her face light up at his presence. And from the look on his, he noticed. Mrs. Perkins stirred and then noticed the handsome detective standing in the doorway. She pulled up her covers to her chin. "Do you have news?"

He hitched his hip on the edge of her hospital bed. "I do. Shannon and Jayden are heading back to Texas. Evidently, they discovered what they set out to find, but unfortunately, they didn't have any luck persuading Manny to come back with them."

"Then they spoke with him? He's alive?" Her pale eyes brightened in color.

Chase shot a glance at Bailey then patted the old woman's hand. "Evidently so. He went through a rehab program several years ago, straightened his life out and got a great job. They can tell you more when they come visit."

She pursed her lips together as if she wanted to inquire further but he cut her off by patting her cheek.

"In the meantime, I have an idea. My parents have a casita, a guest house, by the pool. No one is using it now. They are offering it to you for as long as you need it. The social worker has checked, and your Medicare covers home hospice. You can have the proper care you need and feel safe in a secure, gated community."

Bailey leaped from her chair. "Chase. That is wonderful. Wow. How kind of them."

He wrapped his arm around her waist. She let him leave it there.

"They are headed to Europe for six weeks on a cruise down the Vltava through the Czech Republic. I am babysitting the house and their pet Corgi, Charlotte. So, I will be available. When I am not, I will make sure a patrol drives by often. You will be safe and sound."

Bailey leaned into his hug. She realized she fit his embrace perfectly, as if God-designed. Was this truly the man He had in mind for her? His aftershave, residual from this morning, mixed with his manliness. It stirred her emotions as much as his offer. To calm herself down before anyone noticed, she referred back to the case.

"Any word on who might have given Mrs. P. that overdose?"

He released her, and his warmth dissipated way too

quickly. "Yes. But I can't reveal the details, yet." He rose. "I'll come by in the morning to move you into the casita. The hospital social worker is setting up everything now."

He motioned for Bailey to follow him into the hall.

She told Mrs. Perkins she'd be right back and walked out with him. They stopped outside her door. He kept his voice low. "I didn't want to say anything, but my friend Hartman has obtained the medical records on the last ten patients to have died in that facility. He brought them to my office. Want to comb through them and see if anything jumps out at you?"

She slapped her hand to her chest. "I don't have medical knowledge."

He placed his hands on her shoulders. "I know. But you have a keen mind. You detect patterns and can analyze if something is not how it should be. That's what makes you so valuable at your accounting firm."

His compliment flushed through her. She knew her cheeks must be crimson by now. "Okay, if I can be of assistance."

"It would help a lot. I have some other cases that need my team's attention right now. But I don't want this to slide. Not considering the threat you received." He brushed one hand down her hair. "That hit the personal category."

"Chase." She glanced right and left down the corridors to see if anyone watched their intimate encounter. No one seemed to notice, or care.

His smile warmed as he shifted her chin back to his face. "Which is why I want you to do this at the office, under my supervision. You still have personal time off?"

"For two more days."

"Good. I'll see you in a bit, then." He pecked her on the cheek.

She placed her hand where his lips had landed as she watched him walk away. Now she knew how Shannon's heart must thump whenever Jayden was around.

Two hours later, she pushed on the turnstile that led into the sheriff's headquarters where Chase worked. She recalled the first time she got up the gumption to come ask him to help her locate her aunt after she'd dumped him six months earlier when he tried to date her. It seemed so long ago. Hard to believe it had only been a little over a year.

She walked up the stairs, through the corridor, and tapped on his door. A man she recognized as one of the other detectives waved. "He said the files are down here in the conference room and for you to get started. He had to follow up on a lead." He motioned with his coffee mug.

"Right. Thanks." She followed the man to a room at the end of the hallway.

He opened the door. "Here you are. If you need anything, holler. Restrooms are down the next hall to the right by the water fountain. Bottled water is in the fridge in the breakroom in the opposite direction. Coffee pot's there, too. Though I warn you, Jay made it." He faked a shudder as he raised his cup. A slight burnt-bean aroma emerged from it. "It'll put hair on your . . . oh," he blushed. "Never mind."

Bailey held her giggle until he left her alone in the room. A pile of ten folders sat on the long table. Chase had thought to leave a legal pad and two pens for her as well. Nice guy.

She removed her jacket, set her purse on the chair next to her and sat down. Better get started. This would take a while. She had no idea what to look for, though.

Lord, I need your guidance. Show me what I need to find.

They pulled up to The Better Life Ahead and parked. Two men were raking away some leaves. Jayden approached them. "Bob Morgan in?"

Another man, Shannon recognized as José from the van, came around the side. "It's cool, man. I know them. So does Bob." He reached out to shake Jayden's hand. "Who's your new friend?"

"This is Manny's son."

José's arm stopped midway through the manly-pump. "No kidding?" He released his fingers from Jayden's grip and extended them to Parker. "Good to meet you. I knew your dad."

"Knew?" A harsh tone clouded Parker's response.

Shannon stepped forward. "José means when he lived here, right? You haven't been in touch with Manny since he left."

"Right." José cocked an eyebrow. "Tell him I said hi." His eyes traveled over Parker one more time as he stepped off the porch. "Go on in. I'll get Bob."

The three stood in the parlor. After a few minutes, José returned. "Hey, sorry. My mistake. Seems he left a bit ago to get groceries. He goes to that warehouse club, so he'll be a while. I can have him call you."

A flash of light filtered through the beveled front door glass. Shannon and Jayden turned to see the warped image of the old Honda backing out of the driveway.

Jayden dashed to the door and bolted down the stairs.

He raced across the grass and slammed his hands hard down on side of the car.

Bob hit the brakes.

By that time, Parker, José, and Shannon had run to the driver's side.

Bob sat behind the wheel, his hands tightly gripping it.

Parker tapped on the window and motioned for him to

lower the glass. Bob did so and killed the engine. He edged out of the vehicle.

Jayden came around to join them. "Headed to the store, huh?" His eyes flared in a way Shannon rarely saw. It made her skin crawl a bit. Evidently Bob's, too. He took a step backward and plastered his spine to the car door.

Then Bob composed his features. He turned to José. "It's fine." José nodded as he stepped away and wandered back down the driveway.

When José was out of earshot, Bob turned to them. "Let's go into my office." Rubbing the back of his neck, he walked to the house. Shannon, Jayden, and Parker followed on his heels.

Once inside the office, Bob motioned them to be seated and closed the door. He came around to his desk as if it barricaded him from an angry mob of Huns. Sitting in his chair, he held his hands in his lap. "Guess I have some explaining to do."

Parker leaned forward, his palms pressing on his knees. "You, do. Yes."

"Right." Bob tapped a pen onto his desk blotter. "Parker, your dad doesn't want to be found. Sorry, but he has his reasons."

Parker's Adam's apple shifted in his throat.

Shannon scooted to the front of her chair. "Why?"

"I can't divulge that. He took me into his confidence."

Bob shifted his gaze to her.

"Why did he make up that story, then? What about the money?"

Bob edged back and tented his fingers. "The money was real enough. Though, no, it didn't come from Parker." His chair squeaked as his torso bent closer and he opened a drawer. "Parker, years ago your aunt left you money in a savings account, right?"

"So?"

"So, I gather that had a huge impact upon you."

Parker jerked his neck. "I don't see how . . ."

"You will. You see, it seems a friend of your aunt's, who used to live in Fort Meyers, moved to Tallahassee ten years ago to be closer to her grandkids. She volunteered at the hospital where Manny was admitted the last time. She gave one of the orderlies a note with the key inside of it and directions to the post office. When they discharged him, he gave it to Manny. Manny went there and found some money in an envelope with a note to come back on the fifteenth of each month. He went back the following month and found some more. It nagged at him. At first, he thought it might be from his aunt. That is what convinced him to come knock on my door and get his life straight. One day, on the fifteenth, when he'd been sober a year, he decided to wait and see who left it."

Parker cleared his throat. "He wanted to meet her

again, right? He felt he was ready."

"Yes, and then it hurt him that it wasn't her, but the friend of hers." Bob laid his hands, palms up on the desk.

"Mrs. P. never knew or surely she'd have told me." Shannon knitted her brows.

Bob shook his head. "Apparently she didn't. Manny confronted the lady, and she told him that she had been the contact in Fort Meyers who had arranged with an attorney to open the savings account for Parker there. And, she was the one who had set up the wired withdrawals every month from Mrs. Perkins' bank in San Antonio. That is how the idea came to her. Now she was able to also help Grace Perkins' son."

"Out of loyalty to Mrs. Perkins?"

Bob ran his finger over the papers on his desk. "To appease her own conscience. You see, it was her son who got Manny involved in the convenience store robbery."

"He killed the clerk, didn't he?" Jayden shot from his chair.

"And was later executed by his crime boss for screwing up, yes."

Shannon snapped her fingers. "She must be the one who sent the news clipping three years ago. It wasn't that she found it while unpacking like she said. She'd held onto it."

Jayden's chin dipped into his neck. "Wait. So why

send it to Mrs. Perkins at all. I mean, why make her worry that her son might be in prison for such a heinous crime?"

Shannon shrugged. "Yeah, that doesn't make sense, does it?"

"That robbery ruined my dad's life." Parker rocked back and stared at the ceiling. His face had reddened. His throat wobbled.

The room lay quiet. The only sound besides Parker's deep breaths was a rake scraping the leaves across the grass outside the window.

Shannon rested her hand on the back of his shoulder. "It's okay to be angry."

Bob spoke in a quieter voice. "And she knew it had, Parker. This was her way of making amends, I guess. The two made a pact. Manny promised to stay straight, and she promised to keep putting the money there until he no longer felt he needed it."

Parker rocked forward again. "So why not tell us that in the first place. Why pretend to be someone named Ernie?"

"He changed his mind. He wasn't ready to meet his aunt after all this time. He came to me, distraught, and asked me what to do."

Jayden jabbed a finger at Bob. "And you helped him make up this story?"

"No, I told him I'd encourage you two to find Parker

instead. I'm sorry. I got caught up in this and the more tangled it got, the more I didn't know how to unwind it all. When your friend, Chase, got Detective Burns involved, I panicked. I hoped that by helping the detective discover the truth, it would persuade Manny to come out in the open. Instead, it made him bolt."

Parker narrowed his gaze to Bob's face. "So where is my dad?"

Bob laced his fingers together under his chin. "I honestly do not know. He isn't answering his cell phone. He skipped town, according to the landlord, but left him a month's worth of rent when he cleared out. I guess he decided to disappear."

Parker slammed his hand onto the desk. "Why? To avoid meeting me?"

Shannon jumped at the sound. Jayden reached for her hand and held it tightly. His eyes told her to stay quiet and let this play out. She sucked in a breath and pressed her shoulders into the back of the chair. She half wanted to stay and find out the rest of the story, but a part of her felt they were eavesdropping. Her mind flipped to Bob's calming, professional counselor's tone of voice.

"Parker, it is hard for you to understand and maybe you never will. Your father has suffered a great deal of hurt and rejection in his life. He doesn't handle things well at times. Many of these men don't." He motioned with his head to the ones working in the yard beyond the window.

Parker slapped his hands on his knees and rose. "No, you're right. I don't. I never will."

He bolted out of the office.

Jayden stood, his mouth open.

Shannon bit her lip and searched Bob's face for an answer.

Bob rubbed his forehead. "Take him to San Antonio. Maybe Manny will get in touch with me in a week or so. If he does, I'll try to talk him into contacting Parker. It's all I can promise." He raised up from the desk and held out his hands. "I hope you two can forgive me."

Shannon nodded and took one of his in a shake. She turned to Jayden to see if he would do the same.

He scoffed and left to go find Parker. She reached down for her purse and gave Bob a quick smile. "We'll work on it. It's what God tells us to do."

She walked out of the center, down the sidewalk, and got into the car.

Parker already sat in the back, seat his head turned away.

Jayden turned the ignition, and the three left Tallahassee in silence.

Chapter Twenty-eight

Mrs. Perkins developed a mild fever so the hospital wouldn't release her yet. But she assured Bailey she felt fine and for Bailey to go help Chase find out "what shenanigans were going on at that horrid place."

Bailey had spent the rest of the previous day reading through the medical files. On the surface, all appeared normal. A lot of the jargon she skimmed over, though. She couldn't tell if the vital signs recorded were good or bad, so she stopped to research it. There were a lot of drugs administered that she didn't know how to pronounce. She searched for a few of them on her phone but soon got lost in all the jargon.

From what she could decipher, most seemed appropriate for dying patients whose families didn't want them to suffer. But, had anyone administered them in a wrong manner? She didn't have enough experience to determine yes or no. After several hours, her brain had turned to gelatin, so she gave up and went home.

She'd gotten to the conference room by eight this morning to give the records another glance with fresh eyes. Surely something would jump out at her.

She set down her to-go cup of coffee and pulled the chair from the table.

"Getting anywhere?"

She swiveled to see Chase's head peering through the doorway. Seeing his freshly shaved face made her insides warm. "I'm not sure. As I said, I don't have any medical training. It seems as if the patients were well treated. Maybe their bodies gave up, and Shannon and I worried for nothing."

He tapped the top of the folders. "Bailey. I trust your instincts. If there is something fishy going on there, you'll find it."

She cocked her head. "I'm hoping that by starting fresh this morning something will surface."

"Speaking of fresh. I ordered frittatas and fresh fruit with poppyseed dressing from the deli down the way. Want to join me in the breakroom?"

She chuckled when her stomach responded with a small growl. "Sure. Sounds good."

He held out his hand, and she slipped hers into it. When they got to the breakroom, she gasped. One of the small tables had been set for two. A single red rose, perched in a glass vase, had been placed in the center. Two of the detectives, standing by the coffee pot, snickered.

He waved his hand to shoo them from the room. They shuffled out humming a familiar love song.

She didn't care. "Chase, this is amazing. Thank you."

He pulled out a chair for her, then sat. Laying his hand out on the table palm up, he gazed into her eyes. "Shall we bless this meal?"

She slid her fingers into his palm, and they bowed their heads. Halfway through his prayer, she jolted. "Oh, my word. I've got it."

He lifted his face. "What?"

"The nurse. Mrs. Salvador. The one Shannon met in the hall. It's her. She's the link. She attended every single one of them around the time they died."

"All of them?"

Bailey nodded. "I recall something Shannon told me. She asked the nurse how she did it day in and day out. You know, treat dying patients. Mrs. Salvador told her it helped knowing she was sending them home to be with Jesus. We even commented that her name meant one who saves in Spanish." A tingling sensation spread over her face. "You don't think . . ."

Chase reached in his back pocket for his phone and punched in a number. "Bob, grab Joe. Head over to that hospice center and bring in a Mrs. Salvador for questioning. She's a nurse. If she isn't on duty yet, wait for her. Catch her when she walks in the door."

He pocketed his phone and took Bailey's hand again. "Good, girl. Very good. Sure you don't want to become a detective?"

She chuckled. "Well, maybe a consultant now and then?"

Jayden, Shannon, and Parker pulled into San Antonio as the dawn crested. Shannon woke up and groaned. "Are we home?"

"Almost." Jayden cast a glance in the rearview mirror. "Why don't we stop at the apartment and take turns freshening up before we go see your great aunt?"

Parker yawned and stretched. "Sounds good. I thought you were going to let me drive when we hit Baton Rouge."

"You were out like a light. Besides, I'm the one used to long hauls. Thirteen hours was not a big deal for me."

Their passenger rubbed his neck. "I thought that coffee at dinner in Slidell would do the trick. Guess not."

Shannon smiled. "I crashed, too, didn't I? I vaguely recall crossing the Mississippi River."

Jayden grinned. "You two had quite a duet going there."

She punched his arm. "You're saying I snore?"

He shrugged. "I'm not saying any more."

For the first time since they left Tallahassee, Parker chuckled. Good to hear. Shannon smiled at her man, her heart as warm as gooey brownies straight out of the oven.

He winked, and she noticed his lips curve into a soft smile.

They skirted the city, taking the express loop, and arrived at the apartment just as other cars left to join the morning commute.

"Why don't we let Parker have the first shower. He needs it more than we do. I mean," she turned to their guest with a cringe. "You want to look nice for your great aunt, right?"

He rubbed the stubble on his chin. "Yes. Thank you."

She cleared the embarrassment from her throat. "It's down the hall. Fresh towels are in the cabinet."

He picked up his duffel and headed in the direction of the bathroom.

Shannon entered the small, shotgun kitchen to make coffee. "About all I have is eggs and frozen waffles."

Jayden leaned on the breakfast bar. "Sounds fine to me. It's good to be home."

She smiled, then turned her head so he wouldn't see

her worry. How long would he be home if he didn't find a job soon? Rent was due in two weeks. Could their bank account handle it after all they'd spent in Florida?

She shook it away. *File it back in the God section of your brain, girl.* She filled the carafe with tap water and poured it into the coffee maker. It soon began to gurgle, and the aroma of java beans filled the apartment.

Parker came out, dressed in slacks and a button-down pinstriped shirt. "That smells great."

Jayden waved his hand in front of his nose. "So do you. How much aftershave did you use, man?"

Parker's freshly de-fuzzed cheeks turned red. "My hands were shaking a bit. Splattered it, I guess."

Shannon set the waffles on the table. "You're fine. Jayden's just jealous because he stinks."

Her husband grabbed a waffle, shoved it in his mouth and headed down the hall. The bathroom door closed with a wham and the pipes screeched.

Shannon laughed and handed their guest a plate. "He'll get over it."

Parker chuckled and dug into his waffles and eggs.

An hour later, they piled into Shannon's car, leaving the rental in the visitor's parking area of the complex. "The hospital isn't more than thirty minutes away."

"Is she okay?" Parker's voice sounded nervous.

Shannon swiveled to half face him in the back seat.

"Bailey says her fever is gone, so most likely she will be discharged today."

Parker bobbed his head. "To go to your friend's guest house. I want to meet him and shake his hand."

Shannon righted herself and stared out the windshield. "You will. He's finishing up a case right now. He'll be by later."

Jayden shot her a glance. His face held a hold-your-tongue, girl, expression.

She gave him a reassuring smile. While Parker had been showering, Bailey had called them to tell them about Mrs. Salvador. Parker didn't know his great aunt, or anyone else, had been in danger. They'd decided he didn't need to know.

Instead, she chatted about San Antonio sites as they traveled to the medical complex on the northwest side of town.

They walked down the hospital corridor, weaving through nurses, techs, and other family members visiting their loved ones on this wing. They stopped outside the door to Mrs. Perkins' room.

"You ready?" Shannon touched Parker's arm.

He sucked in a deep breath. "Yeah. Let's do this." He clutched the bouquet of roses from the hospital gift shop in one hand and knocked with the other.

An elderly voice told them to enter.

As Parker opened the door, Shannon peered around his shoulders to see her mentor's face glowing with delight and her eyes swimming with happy tears. A familiar-looking man held Mrs. Perkins' hand.

Shannon gasped.

Parker stopped in mid-step. His eyebrows scrunched together.

The man turned to greet them. When he did, his side-swept bangs ruffled to reveal a small scar between his eyebrow and left temple.

"Hello, Ernie." Jayden scoffed even though a smile crawled over his lips. "Didn't expect to see you here."

Parker dropped the flowers, which Shannon stooped to catch before they hit the ground.

Mrs. Perkins frowned. "Ernie? What is he talking about, Manny?"

The man patted her hand. "It's a joke, Auntie. When they found me in Tallahassee, I didn't tell them I was coming to see you." He raised his gaze to meet Parker's. "Hello, son."

"You're Parker?" The old woman squealed with joy as her hands went to her mouth.

"Yes, Great Aunt Grace." Parker edged over to the bed, tears trickling down his face.

The two men embraced.

Shannon suddenly felt like an intruder. She took

Jayden by the arm and pulled him out of the room. Fighting back sweet tears, she quietly closed the door.

She gulped back the emotions clogging her throat and turned to gaze into her husband's face. "I don't understand how, but I guess we kept our promise after all."

Jayden swept his arm around her waist. He whispered in her ear. "God took care of this. He'll do the same for us, girl."

She smiled and snuggled her head into his shoulder as they walked to the elevators.

The next morning, they got the call. Mrs. Perkins had passed peacefully in her sleep.

Shannon cried off and on the rest of the day. Jayden could do little to comfort her. Bailey and Chase came over, and the two girls hugged and sniffled while Chase and Jayden stood around feeling like third thumbs.

About five, a knock sounded on the door. Parker and Manny stood on the other side, their faces drawn.

"Come in, man." Jayden motioned them inside. "Join the wake. We've just ordered pizza. Jessica and Grady are on their way down from Oklahoma. They should be here in an hour."

Shannon hugged the two men, introduced them to Chase and Bailey and got everyone some iced tea. Jayden figured it helped her get a hold of her emotions by doing something like playing hostess. While she fiddled in the kitchen, he got everyone seated.

When she brought out the tray, he helped her distribute the drinks and snacks while they waited for the food, and Jessica, to arrive. After some initial chatting, Manny cleared his throat. "I have Aunt Grace's will. Her attorney, Mr. Jordan, gave it to us."

Jayden's throat clenched. He recalled what his wife had said about Mrs. Perkins including them in it. "Hey, look. When she drew that up, she had no idea either of you still existed."

Parker grinned and exchanged a nod with his dad. "We know. It's cool. We aren't here to contest it."

Manny reached in his jacket pocket and pulled out a piece of paper. "Mr. Jordan had her jewelry and knickknacks appraised. And her bonds. It seems as if my aunt died a rather wealthy woman. All totaled, he figures at auction they should bring in a little over $1.5 million."

Shannon squealed and dropped her glass. Bailey jumped up and dashed to the kitchen to grab paper towels.

After the ruckus settled, Jayden spoke up. "Of course, we will concede to you, the rightful heirs."

Parker shook his head. "I got my inheritance all those

years ago, and more. Knowing there was a person I'd never met who cared enough to do that set me straight. All my anger for Dad melted that day we learned of her deposits in that savings account." He patted his father on the back. "I realized that the way I'd been toward him was no different than the way he'd been with her. We shared a leave-me-alone attitude, but Aunt Grace's love and prayers eventually dissolved it in us both." He gulped back a sudden shakiness in his voice. "Besides, I have a great job, a good wife, and a decent nest egg building up."

Manny smiled. "I have my social security and a good job now. Plus, all my medical bills are covered by Medicare and the Navy. I don't need much, and Parker says if I ever do, he'll be there for me, so —" he shrugged — "we've decided my aunt's wishes need to be honored. Ninety percent of the proceeds from the auction will go to her church, the Holy Family. The remaining ten percent is yours. It's the least we can do for all you two did to bring our family back together."

Jayden sputtered. "But that's around $150,000, man."

Shannon grabbed his hand in hers, her eyes wide with delight. "Enough to start up your own delivery business and maybe put some money down on a house?"

His eyes filled. "So, we can start a family. Finally."

"You want that?"

"Of course."

"Oh, Jayden." She leaped into his arms as the room filled with claps and whistles.

He held her close and whispered a thank you to Parker and Manny, then to Bailey for getting his wife involved in this crazy family search stuff in the first place. And of course, to the One who had heard his prayers after all and orchestrated this amazing result in ways Jayden never imagined.

He whispered in his wife's ear. "If it's a girl, let's name her Grace. If it's a boy, Ernie."

Her laughter bounced off the ceiling fan and straight into his heart.

.

Acknowledgments

Foremost, I thank God for placing this story in my heart. I hope it touched yours as well. It is a humbling and yet awesome feeling to be an instrument of His design. May my work reflect His glory, be it my fiction or the devotions I write as well as the ones I edit monthly for Power to Change as a digital missionary.

I cannot thank Marji Laine of Write Integrity Press enough for her guidance, pats on the back, and involvement in bringing this novel to fruition as well as letting the world know it exists. She is the best publisher ever, and I am honored to be under contract with WIP.

It is so very important for an author to have a team behind her. So, I also thank my team of supporters who agreed to read and review this novel and then toot my horn. I couldn't have done this without you. Each of you means so much to me. And I thank Katy Huth Jones, my critique partner, for her brainstorming as well as encouragement.

Finally, thank you, dear reader, for purchasing this book. I hope you enjoyed it and will tell others about it along with the other two in the Relatively Seeking Mysteries series, *One Leaf Too Many,* about Bailey's delve into her grandmother's old photo album that led to discovering a family secret hidden for half a century and *Fallen Leaf* about Jessica's search for her birth parents which leads her to investigate a 30-year-old murder. And of course, reviews are always appreciated.

Sincere regards,

Julie B Cosgrove

Enjoy all of the Relatively Seeking Mysteries!

About the Author

Freelance writer, award-winning author, and professional speaker, Julie B. Cosgrove leads religious retreats, workshops for churches and writer groups, and Bible studies. She writes regularly for several devotional publications and is on staff with Campus Crusades of Canada's Power to Change digital ministry as editor and writer for The Life Project. Their websites help to lead thousands of people worldwide to know Christ, one mouse click at a time. Her own blog, Where Did You Find God Today? has readership in 52 countries.

Julie has published three Bible studies, a devotional, two inspirational guides, and has fifteen faith-based fiction novels published or contracted, including two cozy mysteries series, The Bunco Biddies Mysteries and the Relatively Seeking Mysteries. All can be viewed on her website: www.juliebcosgrove.com.

Awarded one of the 50 Writers You Should Be Reading by the Author's Show in 2015 and 2016, and Best Religious Fiction 2016, Best Cozy Mystery 2017 by Texas Association of Authors, Julie was also an INSPY semi-finalist and a Grace Awards Finalist in 2016. She is a member of the American Christian Fiction Writers, Advanced Writers and Speakers Association, and the Christian Authors' Network. She achieved the highest public speaking level in Toastmasters International, the Advanced Communication Gold, in 2015.

Julie is widowed and lives in Fort Worth, Texas where she is involved in mission and women's ministries. She is a murder mystery aficionado—especially British ones—and loves word games.

Write Integrity Mysteries

Haven Ellingson has been stalked, kidnapped, and beaten by Dade. After her escape, he continued to torment her through threats and constant pursuit. Again she was able to break free, thinking the man had finally perished. But he's back, now intent on destroying the life of another young girl and countless, misguided followers. And Haven is having none of it.

Sometimes you hide from your attacker; sometimes you stand and fight.

The mere rumor of treasure can change lives, destroy friendships... even kill?

Alynne's Stone's planned out and predictable life ended when she hurried to her mother's side to support her during a family tragedy. So why would she now have a target on her back? Her father's death had nothing to do with her, but suddenly she's having these "accidents"? How can she stay and support her mom when someone is intent on eliminating her?

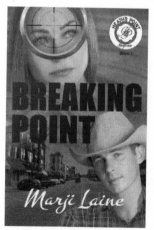

Even in a small town, things—and people—aren't always what they appear to be.

Thank you
for reading our books!

Look for other books
published by

P

Pursued Books
an imprint of

W

Write Integrity Press
www.WriteIntegrity.com

Made in the USA
Middletown, DE
07 May 2021